Before either she or Gus could say more, Leo Thomas, the manager of the smoke jumpers at Redmond Air Field, in Redmond, Oregon, called, "Dana. Good. You're here. Come in my office."

She dropped her pack on an empty chair outside the door and followed Leo. "Hey, my team's ready when you say—" She pulled up short. Her heart thumped hard against her rib cage. The last word stuck in her throat.

Travis.

He rose to his feet from where he'd been sitting in a metal chair against the wall. "Dana. I, uh, hadn't expected to see you."

Travis took the words right out of her mouth. Not planning to see him would be an understatement. The idea of turning heel and running flashed through her mind, but she'd already done that once. She swallowed hard. Grown now, she was determined to act it. Still, words hung in her mouth. The last time she'd seen Travis she'd been foolish er̶̶̶̶̶̶̶̶̶̶̶̶̶̶̶̶̶̶̶̶̶̶̶̶ To make matters worse, no̶̶̶̶̶̶̶̶̶̶̶̶̶̶̶̶̶̶̶̶̶̶̶̶ anything more than stand ̶̶̶̶̶̶̶̶̶̶̶̶̶̶̶̶̶̶̶̶̶̶̶̶

"You two know each other̶̶̶̶̶̶̶̶̶̶̶̶̶̶̶̶̶̶ and forth between them.

She looked at Travis. He watched her. Her attention remained on him as she answered Leo. "Yes, we know each other…"

Dear Reader,

I really enjoyed writing Dana and Travis's story. The idea of a smoke jumper fascinated me. To create a love story in the middle of an adventure only added to my interest. I hope you find the story as exhilarating as I did.

I have to admit I knew little about the important work of smoke jumpers. For my newfound knowledge I have to thank Steve Gray, who put me in touch with Ryan Koch, a smoke jumper. I can't say enough about how much I appreciate his time and knowledge. I admire you and your work.

I love to hear from my readers. You can reach me at www.susancarlisle.com.

Susan

REUNITED WITH HER DAREDEVIL DOC

———

SUSAN CARLISLE

HARLEQUIN

MEDICAL
ROMANCE

HARLEQUIN®
MEDICAL
ROMANCE™

Recycling programs
for this product may
not exist in your area.

ISBN-13: 978-1-335-40439-8

Reunited with Her Daredevil Doc

Copyright © 2021 by Susan Carlisle

This edition published by arrangement with Harlequin Books S.A.

For questions and comments about the quality of this book,
please contact us at CustomerService@Harlequin.com.

Harlequin Enterprises ULC
22 Adelaide St. West, 40th Floor
Toronto, Ontario M5H 4E3, Canada
www.Harlequin.com

Printed in U.S.A.

Susan Carlisle's love affair with books began when she made a bad grade in mathematics. Not allowed to watch TV until the grade had improved, she filled her time with books. Turning her love of reading into a love for writing romance, she pens hot medicals. She loves castles, traveling, afternoon tea, reading voraciously and hearing from her readers. Join her newsletter at susancarlisle.com.

Books by Susan Carlisle

Harlequin Medical Romance

Miracles in the Making

The Neonatal Doc's Baby Surprise

First Response

Firefighter's Unexpected Fling

Pups that Make Miracles

Highland Doc's Christmas Rescue

Christmas in Manhattan

Christmas with the Best Man

Stolen Kisses with Her Boss
Redeeming the Rebel Doc
The Brooding Surgeon's Baby Bombshell
A Daddy Sent by Santa
Nurse to Forever Mom
The Sheikh Doc's Marriage Bargain
Pacific Paradise, Second Chance
The Single Dad's Holiday Wish

Visit the Author Profile page
at Harlequin.com for more titles.

For Mary Beth Norwood, nurse extraordinaire

Thanks for the love you've shown Nick
and our family

CHAPTER ONE

DANA WARREN SWUNG the single glass door of the US Forest Service open with a spring in her step and anticipation rushing through her veins. This would be her time. What she'd been working toward for years. Her boss had called her in. There was a fire burning in the Deschutes National Forest southwest of Bend, Oregon. New, smaller fires needed extinguishing before they joined the larger one. Her crew was next in line to jump with her as their trail leader.

She'd trained for this moment and was ready for the task. Adrenaline coursed through her at the thought of jumping. It was what she lived for and loved. There weren't many women in the smokejumper service, less than 2 percent out of four hundred, but she'd held her own beside the men, earning their respect. Because of that she'd been proud of how she'd moved up the ranks.

Heading straight for the desk of the fire manager, she leaned over his shoulder and studied the computer screen. "Whatta we have, Gus?"

"Nothing for you right yet, but I'm sure it won't be long."

Dana pursed her lips and nodded. Gus wasn't wrong often. His job was to determine the fuel of the fire, the direction, the wind velocity and make the call for the number of jumpers needed to fight it. He was good at his job.

Before either she or Gus could say more, Leo Thomas, the manager of the smokejumpers at Redmond Air Center, in Redmond, Oregon, called, "Dana. Good. You're here. Come in my office."

She dropped her pack on an empty chair outside the door and followed Leo. "Hey, my team's ready when you say—" She pulled up short. Her heart thumped hard against her rib cage. The last word stuck in her throat.

Travis.

He rose to his feet from where he'd been sitting in a metal chair against the wall. "Dana. I, uh hadn't expected to see you."

Travis took the words right out of her mouth. Not planning to see him would be an understatement. The idea of turning heel and running flashed through her mind but she'd already done that once. She swallowed hard. Grown now, she was determined to act it. Still words hung in her mouth. The last time she'd seen Travis she'd been foolish enough to try to kiss him. To make matters worse, now she couldn't seem to do anything more than stand there and stare at him.

"You two know each other?" Leo directed a hand back and forth between them.

She looked at Travis. He watched her. Her attention remained on him as she answered Leo. "Yes, we know each other."

Travis straightened as if gathering himself. "Dana and I worked together one summer a long time ago."

Leo nodded and spoke to Travis. "That's where you got your experience."

"I fought fires during my college years breaks and for the year between college and starting medical school."

Leo nodded, stepping behind the desk. "I see. I bet the medical board found that interesting during your interview."

"They did, and they especially appreciated the wilderness emergency training I have."

Leo nodded before looking at her. "Dana, I need you for a special assignment. I want you to take Dr. Russell to a spot just south of Mount Bachelor. He has a medically fragile patient who has refused to leave his cabin. The doctor fears the man has taken a turn for the worse. To make matters more difficult the bridge on the road into his place has burned and the fire is headed his direction."

Dana glanced at Travis. His blue-eyed look remained on her. She spoke to Leo, "May I speak to you alone?"

Leo sighed, turning his attention to Travis. "Please wait outside for a minute."

Travis started toward the door in one smooth motion. Still as tall and athletic as she remembered, he'd filled out. His jeans fit tightly over thick thigh muscles. He looked trim and fit. Apparently he worked out. Where he had a lanky physique of youth before now his shoulders had the wideness and broadness of a mature man. With his black hair and piercing sky eyes, he could stop her breath. Based on his appearance, Travis looked as if he could handle the grueling physical requirements this trip would require. Something that made up a major part of a smokejumper's life. What she found most disconcerting was he still had the ability to rattle her nerves.

He quietly closed the door behind him. She rounded on Leo, placing both her hands on his desk. If she went on the mercy mission then her team would go up without her. "It's my crew's turn next. This sounds like something for Rescue to handle."

"Your team hasn't been called yet. If they are, Ricky can take the lead. Dr. Russell can't call in Rescue when he doesn't know the medical situation yet. Winds are picking up and this old man's cabin is in the thick of the forest, hard to access. With the size of the fire burning, all the available rescue helicopters are in high demand. He has to assess the situation before he can ask for one. The hope is that you two can get the man out without the use of Rescue. While you're there I'll also want you to form a fire line around the cabin." Leo nodded toward where Travis had exited. "Dr. Russell can assist."

Dana stood straight. She didn't want someone else handling her crew. She wanted to do her job. She cared nothing about babysitting a man she'd made an idiot of herself over. That had been embarrassing enough but being forced to spend time with him again only added misery to pain. "Come on, Leo. You know I've been waiting for my chance with a crew. Can't someone else take Travis, uh Dr. Russell out? My team and I know how to work together."

Leo's eyes narrowed. "There's a man up there on the mountain," he pointed the direction on Mount Bachelor. "He may be old and cantankerous by refusing not to leave when he could have, but that doesn't mean we shouldn't do what we can to save him. The man may need dialysis. You've advanced EMT training. You know the area. You're perfect for the assignment."

"Over half of these guys…" she directed a hand toward the outside office "…can be called woofers because they have the same Wilderness First Responder training as I do. One of them could go."

Leo nodded. "But I'm assigning you to see Dr. Russell gets to his patient safely and that both get back safely. I know this isn't the norm, but it's necessary. You're the best person for the job. You know that area better than any of the others around here since you worked out of the Bend district before you came back here. Dr. Russell assures me this man needs help now or he might not survive. I've given you more explanation than anyone about an assignment. You know what you have to do, do it. Now, open the door and ask Dr. Russell back in."

"Do you even know if he can still jump? I don't need two people to see about if he gets hurt." She didn't hold back her disgust.

"Why don't you ask him?" Leo suggested.

She flung open the door, stopping it just before it hit the wall. As Travis entered, she saw a shadow of concern in his eyes. Did he fear she'd changed Leo's mind? Or that she hadn't changed his mind and Travis would be stuck with her. She glared at him. "When's the last time you jumped?"

"Three months ago. I jump a few times a year. I can assure you that I'm able to manage a jump."

She fired at him, "We've moved to a new system in the last year. We're using BLM now."

"The square parachute. Yeah, I've used it. I don't have a lot of experience with it but I've jumped a time or two with one."

"Good to hear," Leo said.

Dana inwardly sighed. Travis had an answer for everything. Leo fed Travis's confidence.

"Then be here in two hours ready to go. The wind is supposed to pick up this afternoon and a front is moving in."

"I'll be ready." Travis's voice remained firm.

Leo looked at her.

Seeing no way out, Dana nodded and started for the door. She said over her shoulder to Travis, "Be on time." She retrieved her backpack from the chair on her way by, heading for the outside door with hands shaking and jaw clinched.

Exiting the building and reaching her truck, her hand rested on the door handle when fingers lightly touched the top of her shoulder. A shot of electricity flew through her. She jerked around.

"Dana."

Embarrassment heated her cheeks. She looked anywhere but at Travis.

"It's nice to see you again. I'd no idea you were working here. I'm impressed you've stayed with smokejumping. You've moved up the ladder, as well. But that doesn't surprise me. You've always had the brains and brawn for it."

"Brawn, huh? Sounds real…"

"Nice. I always thought it looked good on you." His ice-blue eyes met hers. "Your smarts and instincts have served you well."

His words made her quake. Why, oh, why did Travis still have that power over her? She should've grown up and out of the crush she had on him. Maybe it wasn't that but just embarrassment. What must he think of her? It could only be she was acting like the naive girl she'd been the last time he'd seen her.

She needed to get away. Find a few minutes to regroup before she had to spend the next twenty-four hours with him. "Yeah. I'm still fighting fires. I been working out of this base for three years. I really should go if I'm going to be back in two hours."

Travis backed away. "Yeah. See you then."

As she drove away she looked out the rear-view mirror to find Travis watching her.

Travis had been struck dumb to see Dana. The last time he'd seen her he'd unintentionally hurt her feelings. He'd felt bad about it then, still did. She'd been humiliated and he hadn't known how to make it better. Dana had wanted something he couldn't give. He hadn't been happy about what had happened between them but it had been necessary at the time. He'd wounded a woman's heart he'd called a friend. That was the last thing he'd wanted to do.

In truth, he hadn't kept up with her over the years. But that didn't mean he hadn't thought about her. All the usual stuff had gone through his mind. What if he hadn't had a girlfriend at the time, what if he hadn't been entering medical school, what if they had really kissed, what if…

There had always been something special about Dana. She'd been a great friend and team member that summer. Hard work had been in the center of their time together, but there had been laughter and a comradery he'd not known since. It had been the best time in his life. One he remembered with a great deal of fondness.

Dana had changed, but then, she hadn't. She still acted headstrong and determined, willing to speak her mind. Like before, she had a body to rival any athlete. The physical demands of her job and her growth from a coltish woman he'd known before to the full-grown woman she was now enhanced her appeal. Her warm brown eyes clearly expressed her feelings.

Her thoughts had been clear through those eyes when she'd seen him in Leo's office. Total shock. Travis had recognized that feeling. He'd felt gut punched, as well. They'd have to work past that. Despite their history, he had to trust her to help him get old man Gunter to the care he needed.

A couple of hours later Travis again pulled into the parking lot in front of the large white aluminum-sided building with the long narrow windows, a tall center section and the words US Forest printed on the side. He lifted his medical pack from the passenger seat and climbed out.

He looked around the area at the other buildings comprising the firefighting center. No Dana. He'd parked beside her truck so she must be there somewhere. Starting up the steps to the smokejumpers' building, he stopped when the door opened and Dana exited.

"We need to get moving." She pushed past him. "Let's get over to Cache and get our supplies. The wind is picking up." Stopping at the bottom of the steps, she gave him a pointed look. "Remember, on this trip you take orders from me."

"Yes, ma'am."

They headed toward the building adjacent to the main office. There all the supplies and equipment were stored.

Inside Dana went to a storage locker and started removing equipment. She nodded toward a staff member behind a high wooden counter. "Art can help you with the basics." She looked at Travis from top to bottom. "Tell him not to forget to give you a Nomex shirt and pants. You need to be in something fire resistant."

"Got it." He turned to walk away.

"Wait up. Let me see your boots." Dana stopped what she'd been doing and looked at his feet.

"What's wrong with them?" He picked up one and then the other looking at the soles.

"I wanted to see the heel. You need to be wearing ones with a low heel. None of those fancy hiking boots. Steel-toed?"

He nodded.

"Those will do." Her attention returned to her locker.

By the time Dana joined him he had a bright yellow shirt, dark green cargo pants, a black supply bag and jumpsuit lying out on the counter.

She handed him a small radio.

"I get one of these?" He turned the radio over, looking at it.

"Yes. The protocol changed a few years ago. Everybody has a radio now."

He nodded. "Sounds like a good change to me. It should've been done sooner."

Travis grabbed the shirt and pants. "I'll have these on ASAP." He stepped out of sight.

He returned to find that Art had placed two sleeping bags, fire blankets, cook can, batteries, strapping, first-aid kit, and a collapsible bag for water on the counter along with flares and a helmet.

Dana had already gathered them packaged food or MREs. "I don't need to give you instructions on packing your bag, do I?"

She wasn't cutting him any slack. He gave her a smirk. "No, I got it."

Ten minutes later they were picking up their parachute pack. They each stepped into and zipped up their jump pants. Travis pulled his suspenders over one shoulder and then the other as Dana tugged the heavy matching tan jacket on. She took time to make sure the cone-shaped neck collar stood high. Travis followed her lead.

She gathered her parachute. He took it from her. To his surprise she gave him no argument as he held it for her to slip her arms though the shoulder straps. She did the same for him. They then secured their own leg straps and closed the chest clip.

"Your chest strap is too loose." Dana stepped close.

Near enough the warm fresh scent of female filled his nose. He remembered Dana's smell. If he'd been asked if he did he would've said no, but he recognized it right away as something special to her.

All business, Dana pulled on the strap end until it fit secure across his chest and quickly moved away.

"I do know how to do this."

"Maybe so, but you're my responsibility on this trip and I intend to return you in the same condition as I took you."

He grinned. "So I'll have a guardian angel."

Her eyes rose to meet his. "No. I'm just being a safe smokejumper."

Travis adjusted all the equipment hanging

on him. "I forgot how daunting and cumbersome all this equipment is."

"Yeah, but you'll be glad to have it when we're on the ground."

"Never doubted it." Maybe with a little levity she wouldn't be so uptight. Tension swirled around them. Surely they could coexist for a day.

Travis closed the Velcro of the jumpsuit at his ankles and wrists then clipped on his personal pack to his waist. Picking up his jump helmet, he then followed Dana out the door. They lumbered toward the already running prop airplane waiting on the runway.

"We're going in a Cessna instead of a Sherpa?"

"Yeah. Since it's just the two of us we don't need the larger plane." She stepped aboard.

The spotter nodded and took the large supply bag from Travis before he took a seat on the bench across from Dana.

They strapped in and were on their way down the runway minutes later.

Dana laid her head back and closed her eyes, effectively shutting him out. Travis studied her a moment. She'd let her straight brown hair grow. It hung around her face and bounced around her shoulders. There were lines around her eyes. Had he been a part of making those appear?

In Leo's office, he'd appreciated her simple T-shirt, cargo pants and sturdy boots that might've looked unflattering on another woman but suited Dana. Her clothes had showed curves that had been girlish years ago but had a developed femininity to them now, especially the black shirt that pulled tight across full breasts. He couldn't help but notice.

Did she have a significant other? Had she found the happiness that he hadn't?

The look of devastation in her eyes that day when he'd rejected her had haunted him for a long time. It seemed to have gone deeper than it should have. When he'd told her he had to stop, the life had gone out of her eyes. Sadly a friendship had died, as well.

He'd been so focused on himself back then he'd not recognized Dana's interest. The excitement of starting medical school and his plan to ask his longtime college sweetheart to marry him had filled his head. He and Dana were good friends, partners in a grueling, demanding and dirty profession who'd gotten carried away in the heat of the moment. It was but a second in time, yet it carried lasting power.

It was the last jump of the season for them and they'd just helped put out a particularly difficult fire. They were celebrating when he pulled her into his arms and she wrapped hers around his neck. The next thing he knew their lips were only inches apart. Dana moved and he'd turned his head before their lips met.

Travis had released her and taken a step back. *Dana, I can't.*

Dana's stricken look ended further words. *Oh. I'm sorry. So sorry.*

Pain hung around them like mist on the mountains in the morning seconds before she ran. Before he could say more. The next morning he hadn't been surprised when he couldn't find her to say goodbye, but he was filled with disappointment she couldn't face him.

Maybe he should've handled it differently. Done a better job of not hurting her feelings. Dana was younger than him. He had college behind him she only had two years under her belt. At the time he thought it was just as well. If she was mad at him she'd get over him faster. In fact, he never thought he'd see her again. Yet he'd thought of her. More than once. She'd been an important part of a summer he'd remember in detail.

His focus shifted to her lips. When she'd attempted to kiss him, he'd initially been surprised but soon felt flattered followed by disappointed it hadn't happened. Although along with that came the guilt of knowing he shouldn't have feelings for Dana when he loved and planned to marry another woman.

As close as they once had been, there was more than an aisle in a plane between them now.

Dana's eyes opened. She looked directly at him. "Why're you staring at me?"

He grinned. There was that straightforward attitude he remembered well. There was something about it that brought back those secure feelings of so long ago. He shouted over the roar of the wind and the shaking of the plane. "I'd think you'd be used to men staring at you."

She blinked and her mouth drew into a line. "Men who I work with don't stare at me."

Travis shrugged. "I don't work with you."

"You do for the next day or so. So stop it."

The spotter stood and showed all five of his fingers. He mouthed. "Five minutes."

Travis looked out the small window over his left shoulder. In the distance smoke flumed into the sky. Thankfully the wind blew it away from them. He wanted to get in, get Mr. Gunter out and be gone. The worst-case scenario would be a shift in the wind with nothing but the dry undergrowth and trees as fuel between it and them.

Dana stood and started toward the door the

spotter had just opened. Travis followed her. Hooking her parachute line, she rested her feet on the step. He hooked his as well but waited inside the plane. The spotter tapped Dana on the shoulder. She jumped. Travis soon joined her.

He found parachuting exhilarating. More than once he'd wondered if it was better than sex. It began with the chaos of a wildly beating heart, then the furious swish of the wind in his ears as his adrenaline pumped. Then it quickly turned into the sound of silence, the gentle tug of the airstream allowing him to enjoy the freedom and beauty of seeing the earth from above.

He looked down at Dana. Her light-blue-and-white canopy not far from him.

With his weight it didn't take him long to catch up with her. It'd be his guess she barely met the size limit of one hundred and twenty pounds. Which meant she would carry almost her bulk in equipment when they hiked. She was something else. He had recognized her fortitude years ago but now he'd aged enough to admire it.

He discerned the moment the wind current caught her, pulling her away from him and toward a cluster of trees. Despite the Ram parachute system giving her better control in the burst, the last he saw before he needed to prepare for his own landing was her canopy being grabbed by a limb.

Bringing his knees up so his feet faced the ground, Travis landed on his calves and rolled to his side before coming to his feet. He quickly pulled his parachute down, gathering it in his arms as he went. Moving with knowledge and efficiently, he took off his helmet and unclipped the parachute harness. He dropped that to the ground and loped toward Dana.

She hung about seven feet from the ground. Using her body weight, she swung back and forth trying to grab the tree trunk.

He reached up and could just touch her ankles. "Unclip and drop down. I've got you."

"Let go. I can handle this." She ground out as she glared at him.

He met her unwavering look with one of his own. "We don't have time for you to be stubborn. I've got you. Would you accept help from one of your crew?"

With a huff she gathered a length of a parachute line and clipped it to her jump jacket. "Okay."

Travis went into a stance with one foot ahead of the other. He raised his arms. She stiffened, going as straight as possible before she released the clasp. His hands grasped her waist as she slid through his arms slowing her decent. Dana's hands quickly rested on his shoulders. He rocked back as he held her weight but steadied.

As soon as her feet hit the ground he stepped back and let her go.

She pulled on the parachute. "I've got to get this canopy out of the tree."

"Can't we just leave it?"

She gave him a pointed looked that included gathered brows. "You should know better than that. Nothing has changed since we trained. We have to haul out anything we bring into a national forest. Set an example to the visitors. Also no added fuel for a fire. Plus I'll need it for my next jump after I sew up the tears." She unclipped the line and started pulling.

He joined in the effort as much as Dana would allow. A couple of times his extra muscle helped pull it free when it was stuck. Finally they had it down. Dana rolled it up.

It wasn't until then he saw the gash on her cheek. "You're hurt."

"I'm fine." She pulled off her helmet. "We need to get the kicks boxes open and stow away these jumpsuits."

He'd not even noticed their larger supply bags lying in the middle of the meadow near where he'd landed. The spotter had pushed them out of the plane. Travis caught up with her as she stalked toward them. "No, you're not. Let me have a look at you."

When Dana didn't slow he grabbed her arm. "Let me see."

She jerked her arm away from him. "Please don't touch me." Her eyes grew wide as if upset she'd shown that much emotion. Her voice took an even tone as she said, "We need to get going."

"Quit fussing and let me clean you up." He lifted her chin so he could see more clearly. "How did this happen?"

"A stick broke as I was pulling on the canopy and I turned back and it came through the face guard of my helmet. Stupid mistake."

"It just missed your eye. I'm getting my bag." He went to his supply bag and found his medical backpack. He returned to where Dana removed equipment from her kick bag. After going into his pack he pulled out a packet of four-by-four gauze pads and sterile water. "I'm going to clean you up and see what we've got."

To his amazement, she stilled and presented her face to him. Stepping closer, he went to work removing the dried blood around the puncture wound. He dug into his bag again for a tube of antiseptic cream and a butterfly bandage. "If we weren't out here I'd say you need a small stitch or two not to have a scar."

"That's no big deal." Dana shrugged the idea off.

It should be. She was too pretty to be marred. "I'll try to make the butterfly as tight as possible. Maybe it'll do the trick."

"You done yet?" Her voice held a gruff note as she looked away from him.

"Almost." He secured the tape to her face.

"Good. We should get going."

CHAPTER TWO

DANA GLANCED BACK at Travis as she wiped the sweat from her brow. The hot, dry August weather wasn't her favorite. Yet this was right in the middle of fire season and she did love her job. The one she should be doing if it wasn't for playing tour guide to Travis. He wore a stoic look on his face as they trudged across the meadow toward a stand of trees.

Her stomach squeezed. It was just the two of them. Six thousand feet above sea level in a wilderness. Her life sure had taken a drastic turn. In two days she'd right it. It was only temporary. She'd get Travis back home. After that they might see each other at the grocery store once a year and pass niceties.

She shifted the chain saw sitting across her shoulder. Travis had looked surprised when she'd pulled it out of the bag before stuffing her jumpsuit and parachute into it.

"I was just thinking it was nice not to have

to carry a chain saw and then out you come with one. Are we really going to need that?"

"You never know. I believe in being prepared. I also had Art add some firefighting chemicals." She grinned to herself.

He must've seen her look because he said, "I'd forgotten what it was like to carry all this equipment plus water."

"No complaining, Doctor. You're the one who asked to come."

"I did. I'm just making conversation."

"Conversation isn't necessary." Talking meant she might discuss a subject she didn't want to. She continued walking.

"Why do you mind taking me to Gunter's place so much? I don't understand why I'm such an inconvenience to you."

"I can see why you wouldn't." She wasn't being fair to him and she knew it but couldn't stop herself. She'd been working to lead her own trail crew and instead of that she had this babysitting job, no matter how noble the reason. To make matters worse, she'd been blindsided by Travis returning to her life. Her nerves were on edge and her mind not thinking right. It was too much in one day. "My crew, *my* crew, is going up for the first time and I'm not getting to lead them."

"Hey, I'm sorry. I know you must be disappointed. I remember how ambitious you were. I'm sorry to mess things up."

It wasn't the first time. He jumbled her up all those years ago, as well. She'd wanted to find a hole and bury herself in it when she tried to kiss him. In her excitement she found herself in his arms, a place she'd dreamed of being in more than once. In that weak second she'd forgotten about his life's plans and gotten caught up in the heat of the moment. With the addition of her traitor's heart, she'd made a mistake. Adding his rejection to that of her parents and she'd closed herself off further from others. Just a few years ago she opened enough to let Ryan in and that had got her a kick in the teeth, as well. Not again. She'd learned to let her job be her love. It wouldn't disappoint her. Leave her wanting. "It is what it is."

"I had no idea you were still working out of the Black Butte base."

"I left for three years and worked in Bend to get some experience elsewhere then came back."

There was a long pause. Apparently he'd been waiting on her to say more. When she didn't he asked, "Do you still live with your grandfather?"

"He passed away two years ago."

"Sorry to hear that. I know you were close."

Her grandfather had raised her but she wouldn't have said they were close. He'd done what he had to after her parents had left her with him. They went off to follow their dreams of being musicians. That ended when they died in a bus crash.

Dana walked faster, putting some distance between her and Travis. She had no interest in rehashing her life's story. Her job was to get him to Gunter's place, not to rekindle their friendship. Those days were gone. He'd hurt her; as unintentional as it might have been, it had been another rejection. She refused to get to know him well enough to chance it happening again.

Heading up a rise, she turned to check on Travis. He wasn't far behind. She had to give him credit for that after the pace she'd been setting.

She'd radioed base letting them know their position before they had started walking and gave them the direction she intended to go. Along with that she reported the conditions and asked for a weather report. A front was rolling in quicker than expected. She and Travis needed to keep moving if they didn't want to sleep in the rain or a lightning storm.

"We've a couple of hours walk to Gunther's

land with another hour to the house, I estimate. We should reach him by this evening. If we continue to push on."

"Good, that means if we need to get him out we'll know by tomorrow morning when the weather will be to our favor."

After locating the hiking trail they started north along it.

Travis asked, "Do I smell smoke?"

"Yeah, but it's coming from miles away," she said over her shoulder.

"I like that idea. By the way, where are we?"

She heard him shift his pack. "Fuzztail Butte Trail."

"When we stop I'll have a look on my map."

"Is that a hint you need to rest?" Dana stepped around a boulder and he followed. They were climbing higher.

"I'll be ready to stop when you are."

She said nothing more and kept going. So did he need to rest?

"Dana, tell me how you've been."

Was Travis really interested? They had been such good friends for such a short time and then she'd messed that up. "I've been fine."

"I can see that. I want to know how you've been the last eight years."

Since she'd tried to kiss him. Or since he rejected her and she'd run off? "Why don't we start with you? Are you married with two-point-five kids and a dog?"

"Okay, I'll start but only if you promise to tell me something about yourself."

She gave him a noncommittal unladylike grunt. Why did he keep pushing her about her past?

Travis went on as if she hadn't responded. "Brittney and I did get married. It lasted almost three years. Six months if you really want the truth. Of that I'm not proud. I have no children but still hope for some one day. Now your turn."

She heard the bitterness intertwined in his words. His marriage had failed. Despite her best effort, her heart went out to him. That had to have been difficult for him. Travis had been looking forward to this big, bright future he had planned. She started down a steep grade toward the sound of rushing water. Speaking loud enough she'd be heard, she said, "I finished forestry school. Worked summers as a firefighter while in college then was hired on full time."

"So you finished your Natural Resources Management degree?"

"Yes." Pride washed through her. First one in her family to go to college, much less finish. She'd paid her way through. Her grandfather hadn't the money to help her.

Travis's voice held a note of delight. "See, we're having fun now. I moved back to Redmond six months ago."

"I had no idea." If Dana had she would've been looking over her shoulder whenever she went out. When they returned she'd be doing just that.

"Yeah, I could see that by the look on your face this morning." Travis chuckled. "Small world."

"Yeah, or bad karma," she muttered.

"I finished medical school at the University of Southern California."

The air cooled as they moved closer to the water. "Fancy. I garden when I have time."

"No husband or children?"

"No." Her chest tightened. She hadn't found anyone who lived up to him. Or would stay around long enough to make that commitment.

He quickly came back with, "I live in a condo complex that I hate."

"You never did like being closed in."

"Nope. That hasn't changed." The words came from close behind her.

"What has changed about you?" She really wanted to know.

"I don't see life through rose-colored glasses anymore."

* * *

Travis should have expected this. How like Dana to ask a challenging question. He looked ahead at the woman moving like a warrior along the narrow, packed footpath. She was as sure-footed as he remembered. She moved in and around rocks without any appearance of effort.

And kept him from fixating on the pack on his back weighing him down that held life-sustaining necessities and the Pulaski tool he'd use to stop a fire. He shifted the backpack with his medical supplies hugging his chest. The water bottle that hung off his tool belt drew his attention as it slapped against his thigh. He considered himself in good shape but he'd forgotten the stamina it took to just walk in the wilderness. Even more aggravating was that Dana looked fresh as a spring morning while he suffered.

Even with the misery he moved in, he refused to ask Dana to stop. He wouldn't show weakness. As he followed her lead across the thin, high grass of a meadow, Travis could see how easily it could burn as the dry stalks bushed his legs.

"We'll stop down by the creek for a drink and rest," Dana announced halfway down the slope.

Travis tried not to appear overly grateful. When they reached the creek, Dana set the chain saw down, removed her pack and took a seat on a rock. She reached for her water bottle and took a long draw.

He watched with fascination as a rivet of water went down her neck. His already dry mouth went dusty. They were both hot, sweaty and dirty and all he could think about was watching that rivulet disappear beneath her T-shirt. He shook his head and turned his focus to a bug moving around a pebble.

There'd been something between them all those years ago and he still felt it. Sadly, her personality seemed prickly now. Was that in general or in particular to him? I didn't matter anyway. Dana was the type of woman who would want a relationship that involved security and longevity, something he couldn't, wouldn't offer. His short, disappointing marriage had cured him of that idea.

He found a boulder across from her and removed his equipment. After going to the creek, he went down on his knees and cupped water to splash his face. The frigid liquid felt refreshing on his heated skin. From the physical exertion and the mental activity, as well.

Returning to his rock, he pulled out his water and took a long drink. Sitting, he looked at Dana. She lay back in a stream of sunshine with her eyes closed. Since they'd met again it was the first time she looked peaceful. Was she always wound so tight? He lived like that with Brittney too much of the time. Easy, comfortable was what he was looking for in his life. "How much longer to Gunter's?"

Dana didn't open her eyes. "At the top of the rise should be his property line. From there it'll take us an hour. The walking will be harder because there's no trail."

"Great, that'll give me something to look forward to." He hadn't tried to keep the sarcasm out of his voice.

"We've been making good time. I want to be sure we're there before dark." She opened her eyes a slit. "So tell me why the US Forest Service is making this special trip in?"

"Because I convinced them they'd be saving a man's life."

"Who is this Mr. Gunter?"

"He's just one of those belligerent men who refuses to listen to reason. Who can't accept he's in the path of a wildfire and is deathly ill. I inherited him as a patient when I took over the practice. I speak to him weekly over the phone. He missed last week's call. He has kidney disease. He's getting close to needing dialysis and I'm worried he has already reached that point."

"When the fire grew it left him stranded," she finished for him.

"Yep." He pulled his map out of his pack and moved to sit beside her.

Her eyes widened. A breeze blew a length of hair across her face. She gave it an impatient push away.

"Would you mind showing me where we are? As the saying goes, if you aren't the lead dog you don't see the way."

"Are you calling me a dog?" She glared at him but her mouth twitched at one corner.

Travis sat straighter. It was nice to see Dana's humor return. "I am not. I've been happy to follow but I'd still appreciate you giving me some idea of where we are and where we're headed."

She took the map from him, spreading it out over the rock. Taking a minute, she located a spot and put her finger on it. "We're here. We're going here."

"Thanks." Travis studied the map, memorizing the area. "Why do you know so much about this range?"

"Because I fought a few fires in this area when I was working out of the Bend station and also because I like to hike here when I can."

"Makes sense. Do you know Mr. Gunter?"

"Naw. Just heard of him."

"I know you didn't have a choice about coming, but I do appreciate it."

Dana stood. "It's part of the job. Get your equipment. We need to get moving."

He folded his map, stuffing it into his front breast pocket. "I'll carry the saw the rest of the way."

"I can handle it." There was a bite to her words.

"I didn't say you couldn't but I'd like to do my share."

She looked at him a moment then nodded. "Okay. If you insist."

They worked their way up the slope and out of the trees into another small meadow. The dry grass crunched under his feet.

"There's a chance we're going to get wet," Dana called over her shoulder.

Seconds later lightning flashed.

"We need to get out of this open area." Dana picked up her pace.

Travis joined her. The saw bounced on his shoulder. He was glad he'd decided to carry it instead of letting Dana.

They were almost to the trees when a clap

of thunder rolled and lightning cracked not far ahead. An instant later the smell of sulfur filled the air.

Dana jerked to a stop. Her head popped up, nose going high. She reminded him of an animal sensing danger. He started past her. She grabbed his arm. "Wait. We don't need to go in the trees. It could be moving through the canopy."

"Fire?"

"Yes. That hit something."

She spoke into the radio on her shoulder. "Base. Over. This is Dana." She gave their location. "Lightning strike in my area. Can a lookout see smoke or is there an indication on the monitors of a hit? Over."

Now Travis smelled smoke. It had been years since he'd fought a fire and he wasn't looking forward to doing the job again, but it didn't look like he'd have a choice. He might be out of practice, yet once he'd been a good firefighter.

"Come back, Dana," the radio squawked. "We've a small line of smoke about half a mile from you to the northeast."

"I'm on it. Over."

Dana took the chain saw from him and started moving. "I hope you haven't forgotten your firefighting skills."

She didn't wait for him to rely. Ducking her head, she entered the trees. Travis had no choice but to follow. They weaved in and out of the trees at a speed he would've said was impossible. As they moved, the smell grew stronger. Smoke hung in the air above them.

All of a sudden flames shot up in a tree ahead of them. The tops of two trees blazed.

Dana set the saw down. "I'll get these down. They'll go that away." She pointed ahead of her. "You start creating a fire line behind me."

Travis removed the pack off his back, unstrapped the Pulaski before looking in the bag for his hard hat and eye protection. Those found, he pulled his leather gloves out of his back pocket. Dana adjusted her white helmet and pulled a lime-colored bandanna she wore around her neck up over her nose and mouth. Finding the navy one he'd brought in a side pocket, Travis followed suit.

He hurried to the spot Dana had indicated and started pulling the debris on the ground back until he'd created a three footwide dirt area. The fire wouldn't have fuel to burn when it reached it and would go out. He worked as fast and efficiently as he could. The skill from years ago returned. Sweat ran down the center of his back and across his face but he kept going.

The saw roared to life and soon Dana had it grinding into a burning tree. Minutes later he heard the crack of the tree as it fell away from them. He looked up long enough to see her stepping to the other burning tree and doing the same procedure. In no time it was on the ground, as well. Travis continued digging.

"Travis," Dana called. "Let's get the tops of these put out then we can finish the line and secure the burn."

Dana started delimbing the first tree. She worked swiftly and efficiently. He remembered her being an enthusiastic firefighter but she acted as a well-seasoned one now. No wonder she'd earned the title of crew leader. He really hated she'd be missing out on her chance to lead for the first time because of him.

He stepped to a burning limb and used a flapper to beat the fire out. The wide flexible plastic on the end of a handle reminded him of a broom but was effective. He used his as well until they had smothered the fire. One spot continued to persistently blaze. Travis worked to extinguish it.

A quick snapping sound was all the notice he received before a small burning limb headed his direction. Seconds later it landed across his forearm. He jerked his arm back. A ragged hole with black edges showed in his shirt. He had no doubt he had at least a second-degree burn. Gritting his teeth, he had no time to stop and care for it. He kept moving.

Dana finished removing all the limbs from the felled tree, then cut the tree into short lengths so that it could finish burning within a controlled area. With that done, she shut off the saw. Travis continued slapping while she joined in to help him. With the blaze out, Dana removed her gloves and went down on her hands and knees. She felt along the ground for hot spots. It was necessary to make sure the fire stayed out.

"Continue to work on the fire line," she called to him. "I'll do this and help you in a few minutes." She didn't wait on Travis to agree before her attention returned to the ground.

Sometime later she joined him as he worked the line around the area where the burned trees lay. They operated in tandem. He pulled the ground back and she made the zone wider. By the time they were through and she'd declared the fire completely out, it was twilight.

Dana stopped, took a chug from her water bottle and looked around for any smoke. She glanced at Travis who stood not far from her. "I'm impressed you've kept up your skills."

Travis took a long drink. "I don't think *kept*

is the right adjective. They're more like returned out of necessity. I'd forgotten the energy required to do this job and the adrenaline rush it created."

"Thinking about changing careers?" She grinned, her eyes and teeth extra bright against her soot covered skin.

"Nope. I've found I can get the same rush from taking care of a patient. A calmer, peaceful life for me." He pushed back his helmet before wiping his forehead with his bandanna.

Dana hung her water bottle back on her belt. "If I remember correctly your mother wasn't happy about you being a smokejumper?"

"She thought it was too dangerous." He shrugged. "But what could she do about it? I was grown and needed a job."

"I bet she brags about you being a doctor, doesn't she?" Dana took a long pull of water.

"Oh, yeah. She tells everyone who'll listen."

"And your dad?"

"Him too."

Suddenly Dana was jealous of Travis. He still had both his parents. Would her parents have been proud of her, if they had noticed she was alive? "Do your parents still live in Redmond?"

"My dad does. My mom is in California. They divorced just after I started medical school. They'd been having trouble for years. It was an ugly divorce. I guess it's the family legacy to not have good marriages."

"That sounds rather sad."

He picked up his tools. "It is. But that doesn't mean it isn't a fact. Mine certainly fell into the trap."

"What kind of trap was that?"

He didn't want to tell her. Was ashamed. Disappointed in himself for not seeing what Brittney was. "The kind that looks good on the outside but has no real substance."

"You loved her, didn't you?"

"I did for what I thought she was. Until I didn't. Maybe I didn't know what love was. Who knows? It doesn't matter now." He sighed. "You always had a way of getting me to talk about stuff I didn't want to. We haven't been together a day and I'm spilling my guts." He looked around them. "Will we be at Gunter's tonight or in the morning?"

"It'll be dark before we make it but if you're willing we'll do it." Dana picked up the chain saw and made her way toward their bags. She wished they could talk more. There was a need in her to know more about Travis. She shouldn't, it wasn't her business but despite everything she still cared about him.

He followed. "The idea of having a roof over

my head and being out of the elements has an appeal. I'm anxious to check on Mr. Gunter."

"Then we move on."

"Agreed."

Fifteen minutes later they were hiking through the forest again.

"We should reach the road to Gunter's just after dark. The walking by flashlight will be easier then."

"That sounds nice." Travis shifted the chain saw on his shoulder. He'd picked it up before Dana had a chance after they gathered their bags.

She was in no mood to argue with him and glad not to carry the cumbersome piece of equipment. "By the way, you did a good job back there. I was glad you were there to help."

He grinned. "I'm glad I still remember what to do."

They were still trekking through the forest as the sun set.

Relief washed over Dana as they came to the small, rutted road leading to Gunter's cabin. Weary, she made an effort not to show it. "We only have about half a mile to go."

Travis moved forward to walk beside her as they continued west.

"Why don't you take the lead here?" Dana suggested when she saw the light from the cabin. "At least Mr. Gunter knows you. I don't want us to get shot."

"Makes sense to me." Travis moved a couple of steps ahead of her. "I hope he has something hot on the stove."

Travis wasn't the only one. The emotions and hard work of the day had taken a toll on her. She didn't like being surprised. "Does he know you're coming?"

"I tried to call him but the service here is a little sketchy, but I'll try again." Travis fished out his cell phone and punched in a few numbers.

Dana heard the ringing but no response.

Travis dropped the phone back into a pants pocket. "I guess we're going to have to take our chances."

"On getting shot?" She was only half kidding. With recluses like Mr. Gunter, a person could never be sure what would happen.

"I'll call out when we get closer. Maybe that'll get a response."

They walked toward the cabin with Travis yelling Mr. Gunter's name but there was no reaction. They stepped under the small roof over the front door.

Travis called Mr. Gunter's name again. Still there was no answer. He knocked. Nothing.

After going to a small dirty window, he looked inside. "Aw hell."

Dana rushed to the window.

Travis dropped the chain saw beside the door and opened it without announcing himself.

Dana stopped in the doorway. "Trav…" She saw a man lying on a single-size bed in a corner of the one-room cabin. He wasn't moving. Even in the dim light of a lantern she could see his skin was an ashen color.

Travis dropped his pack to the floor and went down on one knee beside the bed. He placed two fingers on the man's neck to check his pulse. "He's still alive."

Mr. Gunter's eyes fluttered open.

"Dr. Russell. What're you doing here?" the man mumbled.

"I came to get you off this burning mountain." Travis grabbed his medical backpack and pulled it to him.

"You shouldn't have come," the man murmured.

"Nonsense. That's what good doctors do for their patients. Even the stubborn ones. They take care of them." Travis's tone remained even but she could see from his quick actions his concern.

"I'd say you're going above and beyond the call of duty."

Dana would too. She'd known Travis years ago but he hadn't been a doctor then. How different was he? How much had life changed him? What she'd seen in the last eighteen hours had been impressive. Was there more to learn?

"Mr. Gunter, when did you start feeling bad?" Travis asked, the worry evident in his voice.

"Just after lunch."

Travis pulled the blanket back from the man's calf and touched it. Dana could see the wash of fluid under his skin.

"You're retaining fluid." Travis pulled a stethoscope out of the bag. He placed the bell on the man's chest and the tips in his ears. After listening, he wrapped the instrument around his neck. "Irregular heartbeat and shortness of breath. Gunter, you're in failure. This is what I was afraid of. We've got to get you out of here and on dialysis ASAP."

The man weakly tried to sit up. "I can't leave my home."

"You don't have a choice." Travis's firm tone made Dana straighten. He placed a hand to Mr. Gunter's shoulder and had him lay back. "Where's your medicine?"

The man pointed to a rough wood box hanging near the rear door. A large metal bowl sat below it on a stand.

"I'll get it." Dana hurried to it. After opening the box, she scooped up five prescription bottles and dumped them on the bed within Travis's reach.

He searched through them. Selecting a bottle, he removed two pills. "Dana, will you see if you can find some clean drinking water?"

"There's a well outside." Mr. Gunter pointed toward the back door.

Dana nodded. She passed a small potbelly stove with a rocker beside it and a book in the seat on her way to the kitchen area in the opposite corner. Picking up a jug, she then headed out the back door leaving it open so she had enough light to see.

She found a hand-pump well ten steps outside the door. It wasn't something she had much experience with but she knew the basics. Giving the handle three pushes up and down to prime the pump, she held the wide-mouthed jug under the spigot. Soon water flowed. Returning inside, she took a glass off an open shelf and filled it. She went to the bedside.

Mr. Gunter looked at her but spoke to Travis as he helped the man sit up. "Who's the pretty girl?"

"Her name is Dana Warren. She works for

the US Forest Service. She brought me up here." Travis put the two tablets in Mr. Gunter's mouth. After taking the glass from her, Travis offered it to the man.

"Not too much now," Travis told Mr. Gunter. "We need to get some of this fluid off you before you eat or drink anything."

"You shouldn't have come," Mr. Gunter said.

"I couldn't get in touch with you. Apparently I was right. In your condition you don't need to stay here. If the fire makes it here—"

"That's what they say every year. I've lived up here fifty years in the same cabin. It's never gonna happen."

Travis shook his head. "That might be the case but that still doesn't mean you don't need medical care."

Dana couldn't help but be impressed with the even tone Travis used when she wanted to shake the old man for being so stubborn. "This time it's headed your way."

"We'll see about that, missy." Mr. Gunter pierced her with a look.

"The name is Dana."

Travis gave her a warning look. "I hate to put you on food duty but would you mind seeing if you can find some soup or something light for him?"

"I don't want no federal government employee messing around in my kitchen," the old man grumbled. "Can't trust a Fed."

"Well, this one you can. And you're not strong enough to stop her anyway. I hope you don't mind us sharing your food. I'd like a hot meal instead of freeze-dried beef. I'll see that it's replaced when we get to town." Travis pulled a blood pressure cuff out of his bag. "Now lie back and rest."

The old man grunted and did as Travis said.

Picking up her radio, Dana started toward the door. "I'll see what I can come up with but I need to report in first."

"Okay. Ask base to call Rescue. We're going to need a chopper here at daylight."

"Will do." Dana stepped out on the porch to make her call. After a brief discussion she returned inside. "The weather is turning for the better. The helicopter will be here in the morning. We're to meet it in an open field about two miles southeast of here. Mr. Gunter, I hope you have some transportation."

The old man grunted. "A four-wheeler in the shed out back."

Travis picked up the man's wrist and took his pulse. "Not what I'd hoped for but we'll make it work."

Dana turned to the kitchen. As she worked

to put some food together she heard Mr. Gunter say in a loud whisper. "I need to piss."

"That's good to hear." Travis rose from the chair he'd pulled beside the bed. "That's what I wanted you to do to get that fluid off your body. I'd hate for you to die after you've put me to so much trouble to get here. I even had to fight a fire. Let's go outside."

A low rumble of a chuckle came from Mr. Gunter. "Fight a fire, did ye?"

"Yep." Travis helped the man to his feet.

Dana grinned. She had to admit Travis had a nice bedside manner. She bet a lot of women had experience it firsthand. She wouldn't be one of them.

CHAPTER THREE

TRAVIS GLANCED BACK at Dana as his patient shuffled beside him. She'd been smiling, then a stricken look came over her face. What had she been thinking?

She didn't seem to fit in a slot like most women he knew. It had been his experience that women were either interested in money, position or a good time. Some in all the above. Dana had grown up and into her own person. She did a tough job with grit and expertise, and more determination than he could imagine anyone else giving such a strenuous profession.

Yet through it all, he'd caught glimpses of concern for him and Mr. Gunter. He couldn't help but be fascinated by her. He'd like to learn what made Dana tick, who she had become. She hadn't been very forthcoming on their hike. Had something happened to her or had someone hurt her?

By the time he'd returned with Mr. Gunter

and settled him in the bed, Dana had something bubbling on the stove and stood looking inside a mini refrigerator. She pulled out a
block of cheese. Glancing at Mr. Gunter, Travis found him sleeping. He'd let the man do so
while Travis and Dana ate.

Stepping over to her, he leaned over her
shoulder speaking softly, not wanting to disturb his patient. "Smells good."

Dana took a step to the side. Following
his lead she kept her voice down. "It's stew.
I found some cans and opened them. No big
deal."

He took a step back. "It is if you're hungry.
Which I am. What can I do to help?"

"Pour a couple of glasses of water. I'll put
the stew in bowls. I'm going to put one to the
side too cool for Mr. Gunter."

While he did as she asked, Dana sliced
cheese, put it on a plate and placed it on the
small but functional table under one of the two
windows.

As she turned back to the kitchen, she
bumped into him. A zip of awareness traveled
up his arm and out through his body. This reaction to Dana wasn't something he expected.
Hell, he'd not planned on Dana at all.

"Sorry. This place is tiny." She hurried on.

"Functional is the intent, I believe." He

pulled the chair he'd been using up to the table and waited beside it for her to bring their food.

Dana brought their bowls and set them on the table.

He took a chair. His knees knocked hers as he pulled up. Dana quickly shifted hers to the side. She acted skittish about every contact with him. What was she afraid of? He picked up his spoon, filled it. "Mmm…good."

She followed suit. "I wasn't sure how it'd turn out. I've limited skills on a two-eye gas hot plate."

Travis lifted a spoonful to his lips. "Gourmet if you ask me."

"Now you're getting carried away. How is Mr. Gunter doing?"

"Worse than I had hoped I'd find him. I'm just glad I didn't wait any longer to come after him. The fire's the least of his worries."

She placed her hand briefly on top of the burn on his forearm. "Don't worry—we'll get him out tomorrow."

He winced and pulled away. "I'm counting on that. He needs attention I can't give him except at a hospital."

Dana looked down at his arm. Alarm filled her voice. "You're burnt, aren't you? Why didn't you say anything?"

"Because there wasn't enough daylight to spend time on me."

She reached for his hand and brought his arm closer, unbuttoning his cuff. "Travis, you still should've said something." She rolled the material back and hissed. "Oh, Travis. This must be painful."

"I can't argue with that." His lips formed a tight line. It did hurt.

Dana pushed back from the table. "I'm cleaning and bandaging this right now."

"No, you're not. Right now, you're going to finish your food. I'll see Mr. Gunter is fed and then I'll let you patch me up."

"I'll agree, but only if I feed Mr. Gunter while you clean up. Are you in any pain?"

"Only when I think about it." *Which is pretty much all the time except when I'm wondering about you.*

Her brow wrinkled as she studied him. "Have you taken anything for it?"

"A couple of pain relievers a few minutes ago."

She nodded. "Good."

In an effort to get the discussion off him, Travis said, "I'd heard of these remote cabins but I've never been in one."

"Yeah, a number of them were built as fire

lookouts by the CCC boys during the depression." Dana continued to eat.

"CCC boys?"

"Civilian Conservation Corps. They were a voluntary group of unemployed, unmarried males between their late teens and early twenties. President Franklin Roosevelt started the program to put young men to work."

"How do you know so much about them?"

She filled her spoon. "Forestry school. And I like history. I've read a lot about the national forests."

"You really love what you do."

She nodded. "Yeah, I really like my job."

"I like mine, as well. It's one thing I've gotten right."

Dana studied him a moment before she dipped her head to the side toward Mr. Gunter. "I can tell you're good at your job."

"Thanks. I like to think I am."

She looked at him. "The one thing you got right... Surely that's not true."

Travis leaned back in his chair. This discussion had gone deeper than pleasant dinner conversation. "Let's just say that all the plans I'd made outside of medical school crashed and burned. I moved back to Redmond to start over fresh and I don't make plans anymore. I just live and enjoy what comes my way."

"Kind of sounds sad to me."

"Maybe so, but certainly more realistic." That happy marriage, good job, house, swimming pool and kids hadn't worked out as he planned. He'd given up on them. He finished his soup and pushed back from the table.

Despite the conversation turning uncomfortable he liked talking to Dana. It was the most civil and open she had been since they had met again. For once he hadn't had to pry information out of her. She'd maintained a distance between them all day, keeping herself closed off where none of the simple friendship they'd shared that long-ago summer could return. Their chat had consisted of short verbal remarks. He wanted to find that easiness they'd once had.

Dana gathered the used dishes. "I'll see about these while you shower."

"Are you giving the orders now?" Travis kept his tone light as he picked up his bowl.

"I thought I made it clear I was giving them before we got on the plane."

He chuckled. "Yeah, you did. But I think I should be leader now since we're in my patient's house."

Dana stepped toward him. Her neck having to crane to look him in the eyes. Her voice went low and tight, "Maybe so, but I think I'll keep the position."

Travis took a step into her personal space. He could see the flash of hesitation go through her eyes but she didn't move. Dana was strong. She'd gained that confidence since he'd last known her. He respected it. "I tell you what, when we're in the cabin I run the show. When we're outside you do."

"Okay, but I'll agree only after you clean up and let me bandage your arm. I don't need two sick men on my hands."

"Deal." Travis offered his hand.

Dana looked at it a moment as if deciding if it would be safe to take it. Finally she slipped her hand into his. Her palm didn't have the soft, pampered skin of a woman who led the easy life. Instead there was strength and purpose in her grip. The thought he could depend on her ran through his mind. She was the type of person who'd stand beside someone she loved during hard times and good times.

"I'll feed Mr. Gunter while you shower. I noticed a handmade shower attached to the back wall. My guess is that the barrel is full of rain water. Use all you want. We can't use it as drinking water. There's a well for that."

"Sounds refreshing." His mouth pulled. She giggled. The sound rippled through him leaving him wanting more. "Nice way to say freezing cold especially since temperatures can get down pretty low at night around here even during the middle of summer."

An icy shower might clear his head where Dana was concerned. The chance to take grime off would be a pleasure. Fighting fire wasn't clean work.

She moved into the kitchen. "Please be careful around that burn."

"Yes, ma'am, boss."

She smirked. "I'm not fond of that tone."

He grinned. "My apologies but I do want to point out you're giving orders inside the cabin."

One corner of her lips lifted slightly. "I'll try to make it my last one."

As he went out the back door she called with laughter in her voice, "Don't take all the hot water."

He groaned. "I'll try not to."

The tiny three-sided enclosure, the third being the side of the cabin, was situated to the right of the back stoop. He'd bathed in questionable places before, including under a hose but nothing like this. On a platform above his head was a large drum with a showerhead valve screwed into it. The floor consisted of gravel.

After putting his flashlight down on the bench just out of the water's range, Travis stripped out of his clothes, hanging them on a nail hammered into the side of the cabin. He placed his boots nearby. He picked up the bar of soap off the bench and turned the tap then stepped under the water. With a great deal of effort he stopped himself from squealing like a girl and settled for a manly yelp. He twisted the water off then soaped up. Taking a deep breath, he released the water again to rinse off. There was something freeing about taking a shower out in nature. If it only hadn't been so blasted cold. He'd brought his extra T-shirt to use as a towel. After pulling his pants on and leaving his boots untied, he hustled inside to finish dressing beside the potbelly stove.

Dana looked at him from where she sat beside Mr. Gunter. Her eyes went wide and her mouth fell open. "Invigorating shower?"

"That would be an understatement." Travis pulled on his dirty T-shirt enjoying her shocked but interested look.

"I'm proud of that shower." Mr. Gunter sat up in bed, cushioned by pillows behind his back.

Even in the dim light from the two lamps in the room Travis could tell his color had improved. Travis worked to keep his teeth from chattering. "It's a nice shower. I just wish it had a hot water valve."

"It's warm when the sun is shining on it," Mr. Gunter assured him.

Travis turned his back to the stove. "I'll keep that in mind for next time."

"Mr. Gunter, can I get you something before I bandage Travis's arm?" Dana stood with an empty bowl in her hand.

"I need to go outside again." The old man moved to rise.

"I'll help you with that." Travis hurried to the bed.

"I'll get my bag and be waiting at the table." Dana passed him on the way to the kitchen.

Travis helped Mr. Gunter outside. When he returned, Travis settled the old man in the bed, then took the same chair he used during their meal.

Dana had supplies spread out on the table. "Okay. It's your turn to be patient. Put your arm on the table."

"Please." Travis gave her an expectant look.

Her eyes snapped. "Please."

Travis placed his arm where she could clearly see it. She examined the burn closely but didn't touch him. Was she afraid to?

Her lips formed a grim line. "That's a solid

second-degree burn, close to a third. You're lucky it's not worse."

"It would've been if I hadn't knocked the limb off." He liked having Dana concerned about him.

"You should've said something." Her words were a rebuke.

"It wouldn't have mattered. We didn't have the time to stop and see about it."

"Tender?" Her head remained down as her finger probed the skin around the burn.

"Yeah."

"The blister doesn't need to rupture. If it does you'll know real pain." She wiped the area around it with an alcohol pad.

Travis said in a teasing tone, "You do care."

Her eyes flickered up to meet his then lowered again. She pulled in her bottom lip as she worked. Fanning the area dry, she then opened a two-by-two package of gauze pads. She squeezed ointment onto them and laid them over the wound. "When this needs to be changed, you'll want the bandage to come off easily."

She picked up a small roll of gaze and began rolling it around and over the pads until the area was well covered. "I want you to keep this dry and clean."

"Are you sure you're not a doctor, as well?" Dana had no trouble taking control.

"Nope, my calling is smokejumping but I do take my skills as an EMT seriously."

He watched her face. "My guess would be that you take most things seriously."

"What does that mean?"

Travis saw the slight tightening of her lips. "I just remember you were quick with a laugh and a smile. Now, not so much." He watched her. "What happened, Dana?"

She met his gaze. "I don't know what you mean."

"I suspect you do."

Dana made no comment as she finished applying tape to the end of the gauze. With efficacy, she repacked her bag. "I'm gonna clean up. It's a treat to have a place to do so when I'm out in the field. Normally I don't get a bath for a number of days."

"Says the person who hasn't stood under the water that melted from an iceberg." Travis glanced at Mr. Gunter and moved to the stove.

She giggled.

There was that sound again. The one that gripped his middle. The one that seemed to slip out unguarded when he least expected it.

Gathering her personal gear bag and a flashlight, Dana started toward the back door.

"I left my extra T-shirt for you to use as a towel," Travis called.

A few minutes later he smiled when a squeal reached his ears.

Dana stepped into the shower stall, enjoying the full moon which meant she didn't need her flashlight. Travis's T-shirt hung on a nail. She didn't intend to use it. Something about the idea of having Travis's underclothing against her body disturbed her. The warmth of it. His smell. The fact he still got to her.

At dinner she'd forgotten her hurt and found him a charming dinner partner yet sad when he'd spoken about his disappointment in how his life had gone. He'd seemed genuinely interested in what she had told him. Today they had worked together just as they had years ago. What really ate at her was she still liked him.

When he'd come into the cabin after his shower without a shirt on her eyes had soaked him in. Travis may not have been a smoke-jumper in the last few years but he had obviously kept in shape. She tried not to stare but hadn't been successful. It had taken him clearing his throat to make her blink and refocus elsewhere. He had been aware of her interest. That disturbed her the most.

Getting involved with Travis wasn't a path

she needed to follow. They'd only be together until tomorrow. In less than twenty-four hours they'd be back to their own lives, just as it had been before she'd walked into Leo's office.

Stepping under the water, she couldn't help but squeal. Travis had been correct. It was freezing. With teeth chattering and body shivering, she soaped up. The smell of smoke lingered in her hair. One of many things her ex-boyfriend had gradually grown to hate. It took at least three hair washings for the smell to wear off. She kept her hair shoulder length or above just for that reason.

Taking a deep breath to fortify herself, she turned on the tap again and rinsed off. Unable to help herself with the need to ease the cold, she snatched Travis's shirt off the nail and toweled off. It was soft and large enough to do the job. Her hands shook as she pulled on her panties and sports bra, then her T-shirt.

"Oh," she yelped when she stubbed her little toe on the leg of the bench.

Seconds later the door to the cabin opened and Travis came around the corner of the shower. "Dana? Are you all right?"

Travis stopped short. Stood there. She stared back. Why, she had no idea. She was used to very little privacy, knew that her job and her respect depended on it. But this wasn't one of the guys she worked with. This was Travis. A quiver went through her having nothing to do with the water temperature or the cool of the night. Even in the dim light Travis's look said he saw something he liked.

"I'm sorry." He turned his back to her. "Are you okay? Did you see a bear? You yelled."

"I'm fine. I hit my toe on the bench." He wasn't moving to go inside. "You were staring again."

"Men do that when they see a half-dressed woman."

She huffed. "You never noticed before."

"I noticed. I was in a relationship and we were on the same team. Time and place was wrong." There was an edge to his voice.

"I know."

"That doesn't mean I wasn't aware."

Her heart hopped into her throat. Her mind might not have wanted to hear the words but her body sure reacted to them. She'd turned hot all over. "Do you mind leaving so I can finish dressing?"

"Don't take too long or I'll get worried."

Taking a shower may not have been the best choice, especially since Travis's look had steam forming on her body. She wasn't inexperienced and knew enough to recognize when a man was attracted to her. Never had Travis given her such an intense look. She quickly pulled on her pants and slipped her feet into her boots.

When she returned inside, Travis was busy taking Mr. Gunter's vitals as the man dozed.

She quietly put her belongings away. "We need to get some rest. We'll have to be up early to meet the helicopter."

"You go ahead. I'm gonna sit up with him tonight." Travis had pulled the chair back over beside Mr. Gunter's bed.

She took her sleeping bag out of her bag. "You're going to need some sleep, as well."

"I'll say, it has been an unexpectedly busy day."

Dana couldn't remember another one like it. "Wake me at two and I'll relieve you." She rolled her sleeping bag out near the stove and crawled in. Seconds later she shimmied out of her pants and put them in a pile next to the bag. Using her arm as a pillow, she closed her eyes.

"Dana, it's been nice to see you again."

She wouldn't let herself look at Travis yet it took her longer than normal to go to sleep.

What felt like seconds later, the floor creaked beside her. Her eyelids popped open to see two sock-covered feet. Her look traveled up long legs to a gently curved butt over narrow hips to a broad back and wide shoulders. "What time is it?"

"Three a.m."

"I thought I told you I'd get up at two and relieve you." She scrambled out of the sleeping bag then pulled it back up over her hips.

"You were snoring so sweetly I hated to wake you. I got some sleep sitting in the chair."

"Turn around while I pull on my pants, would you? I can do it inside the sleeping bag but it's quicker and easier out of it."

"Sure, I'll put some wood on the fire." He turned away and picked up one of the split logs beside the stove.

"What do I need to watch for with Mr. Gunter?" She finished buttoning her pants.

"Wake me if he develops a fever or becomes agitated."

Dana moved over to the bed as Travis turned. "Take my sleeping bag. There's no point in pulling another out."

Travis woke to the sounds of movement in the kitchen. Through the window the sky had yet to lighten. He'd slept much heavier than he intended. He pulled on his pants while still inside the bag which brought on a groan. Stiffness from yesterday's activities and sleeping on the floor, none of which he was used to, had found a home in each of his joints.

He climbed out of the bag, then stretched his shoulders back and forth. He wasn't used to that type of work he'd done over the last few hours. Apparently he'd become soft through the years.

Dana's back remained to him so he had a moment to study her. There wasn't a spare ounce of fat on her. She'd pulled her hair back at her neck leaving a small stub that stuck out. Some hung around her face that she gave an impatient push every now and then with her hand.

She worked at cutting cheese. Her movements were efficient and minimal. There was nothing fussy about her. A pot boiled on one surface of the stove. She glanced over her shoulder as if she realized he watched her.

"Mornin'," he said to her but looked at Mr. Gunter. "How did things go last night? I didn't mean to sleep so long." Travis rubbed the stubble along his jaw. It already itched. He needed to shave but that wouldn't be happening until he returned to civilization.

"Good morning. Breakfast will be ready in a few minutes. I'm warming up something for Mr. Gunter."

Travis took a second to check on his patient, grabbed his shirt then stepped out the back door. He returned with his face washed, shirt buttoned and tucked in. Sitting beside Mr. Gunter, who could hardly keep his eyes open, Travis checked his vital signs.

Dana joined him with a bowl in her hand. "Left over stew broth. He did pretty good last night. Slept through me checking on him."

"Good. I'll take care of feeding him." Travis took the bowl from her. "You eat."

For once she did as he suggested. Mr. Gunter ate hardly anything.

Dana finished her meal. "I'm going out to talk to base to confirm the rendezvous point."

"If I'm not here when you come back in, I'm out back seeing about the ATV." He could eat later.

Travis had the machine started when Dana came around the side of the house. He turned it off and checked the gas and oil. "I've been thinking if I can find a couple of boards to lay across the basket and strap them to it, then put the mattress of the bed on top of that, we could get him down the road easier. Maybe cover them with our sleeping bags because they're warmer than his blankets."

Dana came to stand across the four-wheeler from him. "Sounds like it would work."

"This isn't going to be a fun ride for him."

Travis added a sarcastic lift to the corner of his mouth. He looked around for boards but seeing none, he started toward the back of the shed.

"It'll be better than walking." Dana followed him.

"Can't argue with that. Either way it has to be done. The fluid is building up in his body to a dangerous point. I doubled his meds."

Behind the shed he found a stack on rough old lumber. "These'll have to do." Picking up two boards, Travis carried them to the four-wheeler and laid them across the wide but low metal basket behind the seat. "I'm worried we can secure them tight enough."

"How about nailing cross boards and using them to hold it in place," Dana suggested.

"That would work," he looked around, "if we can come up with nails, hammer and a saw."

"Surely he has those around here some-where. Would have to have them to survive up here by himself." Dana walked farther in-side the shed.

Travis followed. By the time he came to stand beside her, Dana had found a handsaw. She pulled a rusty can toward him. "You find a hammer and I'll meet you outside."

"Okay." He found a hammer lying on the bench and headed to the four-wheeler.

Dana passed him. "I'll get another board. We need to be getting on the way. The helicopter can't wait, especially if the wind picks up."

"Is that supposed to happen?"

She called over her shoulder. "Yeah. And we need them to get all three of us on board."

A minute later she returned with a board in hand. He took it from her and measured the width against the wood they already had. He quickly cut the two boards required. Positioning the cross boards so they sat the distance of the sides of the basket. He hammered the nails into place while Dana held the boards. After flipping the platform over, they put it in the correct spot.

"Now all we need is some rope or straps," Dana announced with her hands on her hips.

"I saw rope in the shed. I'll get it." Travis headed into the shed, soon returning.

Together they wrapped the rope around the platform so it wouldn't move backward or forward.

Pleased, Travis stood back. "Looks good."

"I'll put the tools away. You get Mr. Gunter." Dana gathered the tools.

Travis headed inside the cabin. "Mr. Gunter, we need to go."

The man opened his eyes.

"I need you to sit in the rocker for a few minutes. Can you do that?"

"Sure I can. Can even walk there." The older man moved to sit up.

Travis helped him. In reality the man didn't even have the strength he thought he did. While helping Mr. Gunter, Travis heard the engine of the ATV roar as Dana moved it around to the front of the house. Travis settled Mr. Gunter, then picked up the mattress and carried it outside. Laying it over the boards, Travis returned for Mr. Gunter.

Dana gathered their bags and carried a load out ahead of him. She waited beside the four-wheeler. "I'll help you get Mr. Gunter on."

Together they half lifted, half pushed Mr. Gunter up on the mattress.

Dana had already laid out one of the sleeping bags. She returned to the cabin while Travis covered Mr. Gunter with the other sleeping bag. Dana came out with the last of their bags in hand. Dana gave him his packs, then she fixed hers across her chest.

Travis placed one large bag in front of the steering wheel. The other would ride between the driver's legs. They tied the sheet off the bed to the back side of the basket and to the front, making Mr. Gunter as secure as possible. Done, Dana picked up the chain saw.

"Put that between Mr. Gunter's feet. You drive. Your legs are shorter and you can sit farther up. I can hold the saw with one hand." He climbed on. "This is gonna be a tight fit."

Dana pursed her lips, her eyes holding a determined look. She took her seat, her hips fitting tightly against his and her back pressed along his chest. Her hair brushed his chin, a few strands getting caught in his stubble.

"Ready?" Dana asked.

"Ready." Travis placed an arm around her waist to support himself when she took off.

On a deep exhale, she turned the key and started the four-wheeler.

Travis couldn't deny being aware of Dana pressed so close yet it wasn't something he planned to act on. He'd hurt her once and he wouldn't do it again. He wasn't that guy she'd once thought he was. Life had hardened him.

Despite the bumpy ride, Dana tried to keep the four-wheeler out of the ruts with little success. Her concentration remained on the road, hoping to lessen the difficult ride for Mr. Gunter. It made the trip slow going. She glanced at her watch. It would be daylight soon. They couldn't miss the helicopter.

They were traveling through a tunnel of large timber, tall enough to block out most of the morning light. She glanced up to see the wind blowing the tops of the trees. The motor drowned out the sounds of birds or animals making their morning movements. What she did know about was the heat of Travis's body pressed against hers.

The whole scenario of the day before, and this morning, was something she wouldn't have imagined in her wildest dreams. She tried not to think about Travis and focused on her job. She'd promised herself never to let another man get into her head like her ex-boyfriend had, or before him, Travis. She couldn't let another person hurt her. It was too scary, too difficult, too much work to function again. She'd hold her emotions close and concentrate on her job and the satisfaction she received from doing it well. So far that had worked. Travis showing up again wouldn't change anything.

They came to a spot where they needed to ford a creek. "Hold on to Mr. Gunter. There's no good way to cross the rocks."

Travis removed his hand from around her. Apparently he now had both behind him, one holding Mr. Gunter.

"How much farther?" Travis asked, his hand returning to her waist. His mouth lay close enough his lips brushed her ear.

Just a few more miles, then a ride home and Travis would be gone.

"Not too much."

Dana kept them moving at a slow, steady pace. Wind having nothing to do with the movement of the ATV buffeted them. She raised her head. The slightest hint of smoke filled her nose. Was the fire moving faster?

"Smoke."

Travis had smelled it too.

Thankfully the narrow strip of road smoothed out and she increased her speed. Soon they left the woods riding into a meadow. The space would be large enough for the rescue helicopter to lower a basket to get Mr. Gunter but not great enough to land. Being in a dense area of the forest with no other roads made rescues problematic.

Dana blinked, adjusting her sight as they came out of the dimness of the trees into the bright sunlight. She pulled into the center of the field and turned off the engine.

The whop-whop of blades announced the helicopter flew nearby. *Good timing.*

Climbing off the four-wheeler, she made sure she didn't rub against Travis any more than necessary. She radioed the helicopter pilot, letting him know they were in place. As she did so she watched Travis remove the sheet securing Mr. Gunter.

The man's skin had gone ashen again but his eyes were open.

"They're sending a basket first," she called out to Travis.

He nodded and returned to checking his patient's vitals.

Moments later the helicopter came down to treetop level and hovered over the center of the field. A human-size metal basket was lowered. It swung wildly in the wind. Dana reached out to catch the basket just as it swayed away. Seconds later it rocketed toward her. Strong arms grabbed her and jerked her out of the way.

"Are you trying to kill yourself? I don't need two patients!" Travis's words shot like bullets as they stumbled backward. He finally brought them to a standstill well out of range of the basket.

He released her as the basket bounced against the ground. "Let's get Mr. Gunter on this thing before the weather turns worse."

Together they lifted the man off the ATV. With the support of Travis on one side and her on the other, they managed to get their patient lying in the basket. Travis placed the enclosed blanket over Mr. Gunter. Dana saw to it the straps were secured over him.

Mr. Gunter looked first at Travis and then to her. "My cabin?"

"It'll be fine," Travis assured him.

"It's all I have." The old man reached a hand out, his rheumy eyes pleading.

The radio squawked. "We need to do this. The wind's picking up."

"We're ready down here. Pull him up." Dana said into the radio. She and Travis stood back allowing plenty of room.

The basket swung once so violently she feared for Mr. Gunter. The basket had just been pulled inside when the wind lashed the helicopter pushing it to the right.

"We can't hold here any longer." The pilot voice came over the radio. "Sorry. You'll have to return to base."

Dana's chest tightened with anxiety as she watched the helicopter disappear over the top of the trees and into the horizon. She glanced a Travis. They'd be together longer than she'd anticipated or wished.

CHAPTER FOUR

TRAVIS CONTEMPLATED THE fact that his and Dana's ride out of a burning forest had just flown away. This trip had turned into more than he'd bargained for in more ways than one. He looked at Dana. She'd been completely unexpected. They'd be spending even more time together.

"Understood." Dana spoke into the radio. Her voice filled with disappointment. Her gaze met his.

She didn't look any happier about the situation than he was. He had a practice he needed to get back to. One night roughing it was one thing, two was another. Losing days of work for one patient hadn't been his idea.

She took a few steps back and said flatly into the radio, "Base, it's Dana. The wind has increased. Rescue couldn't pick up Dr. Russell and me. We're returning to Gunter's cabin. We'll secure it and walk out."

"Ten-four," came back over the radio. "Be advised the fire has turned."

"Ten-four. What's the weather report?"

Base came back. "By evening, front should have passed through. It should be a calm night."

"Ten-four. I'll check in again this evening."

"Ten-four."

Travis ran a hand through his hair. "I guess we're in for a hike."

"Yep. You up for it?"

He shrugged. "I don't think I have a choice."

"You don't. Let's get busy securing Gunter's cabin." She started toward the ATV. "Then we'll be on our way out."

"I'm driving back," Travis announced.

Dana whirled to face him. "Don't think you're going to start giving me orders."

He took a step toward her. "All I want is to do the driving."

"You can ask instead of giving an order," she snapped back.

"I didn't realize I was giving an order. You don't always have to have the final word in a situation."

For a second she looked as if he'd slapped her, then she glared at him. "It sounded like an order to me."

Travis walked back to the ATV. "Instead of

standing here arguing let's get started back. If that fire picks up again I want to be hell and gone from here."

A contrite look came over Dana's face before she hung her head. "I'm sorry. You didn't deserve that pettiness. This situation has taken on a life of its own. We're both on edge."

"I have to say life is more interesting around you." To Travis's surprise there was some real truth to that. Compared to the last twenty-four hours, his world looked dull. Being out of the norm added some spice to his ordered, comfortable life.

Dana came over to him. "Let's go. Thankfully right now the fire isn't nipping at our heels and I want to keep it that way. You can drive."

"Sounds like a solid plan." Travis slung a leg over the ATV and settled on the seat.

Dana placed a hand on his shoulder and slid up behind him. He started the ATV. As they rode over rough terrain, Dana grabbed the sides of his shirt. Despite the distance, Dana never relaxed. He felt the tension in her body as if she feared any contact between them.

At one time they had been friends. Shared a companionship that he'd never had with another woman. After what had happened between them years ago he didn't expect her to let go completely of her animosity, but by now he wouldn't have thought she'd still be hanging on to it so tightly. They needed to clear the air. Ease the strain between them.

The return trip went much faster. He pulled up to Mr. Gunter's cabin. Dana climbed off the ATV as soon as he stopped.

Travis turned on the seat. "About what happened years ago—"

"That was my fault. A silly girl-crush." She started toward the back of the ATV.

He continued to watch her. "Please look at me, Dana."

She finally did.

"I didn't think it was silly."

"I embarrassed myself and you. I shouldn't have tried to kiss you. I shouldn't have put you in that position. I knew you had a girlfriend."

"Hey, it was a heat of the moment thing. I was flattered." After he got over the initial surprise.

He knew what being unfaithful did to a relationship, since his father slowly killed his mother with his extramarital affairs. Travis promised himself he'd never do that to someone he loved. It caused too much damage and pain. Being faithful had been important to him. That's why it had crushed him so when his ex-wife had run around on him.

"We were friends and I ruined that." She removed the chain saw from the back of the four-wheeler.

"I should've done a better job of letting you down. I've always been your friend."

She said over her shoulder, "It's all good."

He stepped off the ATV. For some reason it really mattered to him that they returned to that friendship of old. "Is it? I'd like it if we could still be friends."

"We can try. Right now, though, we need to get started on securing this area. I can't guarantee the cabin won't burn but we can at least give it a chance. You start on a fire line. I'll cut back the brush. Less fuel we give the fire the better." She raised her head. "What we need to do is hope the wind doesn't pick up. If it does it won't matter what we do."

Dana had gone into smokejumper mode. Had closed him and their discussion off.

"You start in the shed. See if there're any gas cans or flammables. What we don't need we'll bury along with anything else inside that might survive. We'll water down what we can, the best we can. Maybe that'll stop the worst of it. I'll stay in touch with base for the latest weather changes. That should give us a day's worth of work. If all remains as is, we'll stay

SUSAN CARLISLE

here tonight and start out tomorrow morning. If not, we'll have to hotfoot it ahead of it."

He stood straighter. "Yes, boss."

Dana pursed her lips, giving him a contrite look. "We agreed that when we're outside I'm the boss. Let's get started. I'll start cutting back brush." She didn't give him time to respond before she started checking the chain saw. "Bring any gas or oil you find and leave it here for me. I may need it."

Travis started around the cabin. Dana knew her job.

"Hey, Travis, take the four-wheeler with you."

"We can't ride it out?"

She shook her head. "The terrain is too rough. No roads. Only footpaths. If we're lucky. We'll be making our own path most of the time. Put it under the shed and see if you can syphon the gas out."

"Will do."

He had some difficulty finding a hose to use to remove the gas but he finally found a piece of rubber tubing on a shelf in the back of the shed. With a gas can sitting on the running board of the ATV ready, he put one end of the tube in the gas of the ATV and the other in his mouth. He sucked.

"Travis!" Dana's high pitch scream filled the air.

Gas entered his mouth and he quickly spit it out as he ran toward the front of the cabin where he'd last heard the sound of the chain saw. He slid to a stop. A large rattlesnake sat curled in front of her with its head reared high and its tail rattling. Dana stood back against a large tree. If she moved the snake could strike her.

Her attention didn't leave the snake. "Help me, Travis."

The desperation in her voice went straight to his heart and seized it. She depended on him. This tough woman must be deadly afraid of snakes to have that begging note in her voice. "Don't move."

A limb she'd just cut lay nearby. He snatched it up and slowly dragged it over the ground, distracting the snake from Dana. "Slowly move behind the tree."

Keeping her back to the tree, Dana stepped around it and to safety.

Travis dropped the limb and took a wide path around the rattler until he reached Dana. Her eyes were wide with fear and she shook. He reached out his hand and she took it. They slowly moved away from the area.

As soon as they were out of harm's way she

removed her hand from his. She stood with her eyes closed taking heaving breaths. Her eyes opened. Panic still hung there.

Without thinking, he gathered her into his arms. She trembled. To his amazement she hadn't pulled away. She'd truly been terrified.

With a shuddering breath so bottomless that he felt it all the way through him, Dana stepped back and squared her shoulders. "I'm okay now. Thanks for helping out. I hate snakes. As far as I'm concerned they're the worst part of my job."

"No problem." He glanced around the tree to the snake. "It was a big one. Mean too. We'll give it a few minutes to move on."

Dana's gaze finally met his. "I'd appreciate it if you didn't say anything about how silly I acted to anyone. I just really hate snakes."

His brow wrinkled as he looked at her with astonishment. "You're afraid someone will make fun of you?"

Dana nodded, then moved away.

She was that vulnerable? That afraid to show she had a weakness? Why did she believe she must be strong all the time? He followed her. "I remember how hard you worked to prove yourself during training. Do you remember how difficult and scary it was the first time you jumped off the tower during jumper training? We talked about it afterward."

"Yeah."

"But that first real jump had been invigorating. There has never been anything like it since. I remember the huge smile on your face when you landed just after me." Dana's face had been brilliant with excitement and exhilaration. Even now he could still picture it. He wanted to see that look again.

Her face took on a soft smile. She glanced at him and it disappeared. "We need to get back to work."

Had he hurt her so much that summer that she didn't want to remember anything about it? That saddened him deeply. He headed toward the shed. "You do know that ignoring something doesn't mean it goes away."

She grinned. "Like you?"

Travis sighed. That was more like it. The Dana he liked so much. "Yeah. I does seem like we're stuck together for a while." He went to the shed with a grin on his face.

He finished with the ATV and securing the shed, then started on the fire line. It would require hours of backbreaking work. They took a breather around midday and returned to work again. Afterward Dana joined him on the fire line.

When they were done Dana said, "Now we need to take care of the rest of the things around the cabin. We need to get the flammables buried."

"You keep piling on the excitement." He grinned and slung the Pulaski over his shoulder. "You sure know how to show a guy a good time. I'll start digging a hole."

Dana had to give Travis credit for being a good sport. He could be making the experience more difficult. She'd sure been glad to see him when she'd been cornered by the snake. They had a way for making her brain shut down. It had felt good to have his protective arms around her. She had needed them for a few minutes.

Two hours later, when she came around the side of the cabin, she found Travis on the porch with glasses of water in his hands.

"Here, you need this." He handed her a glass and sat on the bench under one of the windows. "I have the hole you requested dug."

"Great, but before you get too comfortable we still have to water down what we can."

"You keep this up and I'm going to ask to be the outside boss."

"Sorry. We've already agreed on the boss division." She gulped down the water. "I'm going to check the perimeter to see if there's anything else we need to do. I'll also talk to base while I'm doing that." She put down the glass.

"I'll start filling the hole."

"Okay. I'll be done out here in a minute and start on the inside."

"Base, this is Dana." She called as she walked away. "Can I get a weather report? Over."

Static filled the air before a male voice came on. "It's still looking calm for the night."

"What about the fire?"

"Still headed your direction. But fifty percent under control."

"Ten-four. We're staying put tonight. Will head out tomorrow morning on Coyote Loop Trail toward Bright Light lookout cabin."

"Ten-four. Stay safe."

"Will do."

Dana found Travis standing over the hole he'd dug.

He leaned on a shovel handle. "I was waiting to see if you need to put anything else in it before I cover it."

"Nope. If you have all the flammable stuff in there then I say cover it."

"Is there anything else we need to do?" Travis filled the shovel with dirt.

"I still need to sort through Mr. Gunter's food supplies and see if there is anything light enough for us to carry. We didn't bring enough food for the extra days we're going to be out. We have at least three days of walking ahead of us." She looked off at the sky over the top of the trees. It would be dark in a couple of hours.

"Did you get that weather report?"

"Yeah." She told him what base told her.

Travis continued to dump dirt over the items in the hole. "That sounds like good news."

"It was. We'll stay here tonight after all."

"I like that idea. I'd rather sleep with a roof over my head. Just in case there is rain."

She turned toward the cabin. "We'll leave at daylight and make our way as far and fast as possible."

"I'll be ready." Travis picked up his pace with the shoveling.

Forty-five minutes later Travis joined her inside the cabin. He took a seat in one of the chairs with a groan. He rubbed his lower back.

Dana winced, then turned to look at him from where she stood in the kitchen. "You okay?"

"You better not laugh at me. I'm not used to so much manual labor."

Dana had to admit Travis had been a hard worker, sharing the load and following her lead—most of the time.

She smiled. "You don't look out of shape."

"Thank you. Have you been checking me out?"

Dana snorted. She had been, but she wouldn't let him know that. "What're we in? High School."

He harrumphed. "If we were I'd be too tired to make a pass at you."

As if he really would. "I'm going to take a shower before dinner."

His brows rose. "Is that your way of telling me to cook?"

"Not really. You're welcome to see to the food if you wish. If you don't, I will."

He pulled his feet back when she started to step across his legs. "You saw to dinner last night—it's only fair that I do it tonight."

She looked at him her eyes wide with astonishment. "Thanks for that. Some guys still don't think that way."

A spot in the center of Travis's chest warmed.

A few minutes later while busy in the kitchen he heard her yelp. She'd apparently stepped under the water. He grinned. His smile quickly disappeared when the picture of her naked in the outdoors slid into his mind. That wasn't a thought he needed to let take hold. He swallowed hard and kept applying all his attention to putting something for dinner on the table.

They weren't young adults any longer. If he kissed her now it wouldn't be so easily put behind them. He didn't want to hurt Dana. But he had nothing to give her. She deserved better than a fling because they were alone in the wilderness. But that was all he was offering these days. He'd tried for a real relationship and failed at it, miserably.

Travis looked Dana's way when she entered the cabin. All his earlier convictions disappeared like a sprinkle of rain against an uncontrolled fire. Her flushed face fresh from scrubbing and her hair hanging damp around it made her look younger than her years. Dana didn't need makeup to make her attractive. She had a sparkle of life about her that made him want some of it for himself. To absorb it. Feast on it.

Come to think of it, he'd not known that feeling since the summer they had spent together. Somehow he'd been going through the motions. Being around Dana made him want to grasp life and squeeze all he could out of it.

He stepped toward her but stopped. A cold shower would be good right about now. He gathered his stuff. "We'll eat after I get a shower."

"Then I'm going to rebandage your arm."

He said over his shoulder without slowing down, "And I need to see to your face."

"What a pair we make. Not even together twenty-four hours and we both have injuries."

Yeah, and he had other issues, as well.

As the cold water flowed over his back, he moved his head from side to side then rolled his shoulders. What would they feel like after another two days? At least his body aches and pains helped keep his mind off the uncomfortable thoughts he had toward Dana. Those had to stop. Dana sat at the table with sandwiches and soup waiting by the time he reentered the cabin.

They ate with little discussion then cleared the table.

With that done, Dana pulled out her first-aid kit. "How's your arm?"

"Sweating didn't do it any favors." It had stung all day.

Her eyes softened. "I don't imagine it does."

"I gave it a good wash. With a new bandage I think I'll be good to go. And a couple of pain relievers."

"Let me have a look before I cover it."

He held his arm up in the air with the bent elbow resting on the table. She took his hand, brought it down to her eye level. He tried not to let her touch affect him but just a simple nonsexual one had him wishing for more. Did Dana have any idea what she did to him?

Her eyes flickered up to meet his. Heat flashed in them before she let go of his hand. She straightened. In a firm voice she said, "Hold it up again."

He did as he was told, never taking his eyes off her.

She looked at him, but defiance and determination rested in her eyes now.

Disappointment filled him. He'd believed they had gotten past that since they'd returned to the cabin. Found some of their way back to what they had once had. But of course their time together now wasn't any different than what they'd shared before. It was only temporary.

With a gentle touch Dana smoothed the salve over the burned area. "This'll have to hold for as long as possible. I don't have much left."

"I have some in my pack but I'll keep my shirt sleeve down all the time. That should help protect it." He watched as she reapplied a bandage. "Tell me, are you still living on your grandfather's ranch?"

"I am. I don't plan to ever move." She carefully wrapped his arm.

He looked at the top of her head. Her hair

had dried. He wanted to touch it, but wouldn't. "I remember you saying how much you loved it.

"Is there anyone special in your life?" Maybe it wasn't his business but he wanted to know and didn't have another way to find out without asking.

Her gaze flicked up to his then down again. "No. Let's just say that I have a tendency to intimidate men."

He sat back and grinned. "Now there's a surprise."

Dana's gaze, darkened now, met his. She wasn't sharing his humor. "I'm sorry. That's obviously a sore spot. Will you tell me what happened?"

"My last boyfriend started to make suggestions I should find another job. That I was gone too much. He wanted me to go to work in the office. He had a problem with jealousy. Didn't like me being out overnight with other men even though it was part of my work." She huffed. "As if we weren't worn out at the end of the day and just hoping we had a chance for eight hours of sleep."

"So why were you with this jerk anyway?" For some reason he was far more indignant on her behalf than he should have been.

Her fingers stopped moving and she looked

at a spot on the other side of the room. She shrugged. "I met him just after my grandfather died. He worked in the probate office at the courthouse. I had taken some papers in. He was nice. Asked me to dinner." Her mouth twisted into a grimace. "You don't want to hear this."

"I do, if you want to tell me."

"It was a long time ago." She went back to work with the bandage.

Like it had been between them. It shouldn't, but it sort of hurt that Dana hadn't pined for him all this time.

"At first he was fascinated by my job. He told all his friends he was dating a smokejumper. If we were out with a group he wanted me to tell stories. But slowly he started to make barbed remarks. When I didn't agree with something he accused me of being controlling."

Now he understood why she hadn't liked him accusing her of being bossy.

"By that time I was moving up the ranks and he hadn't gotten a promotion he thought he deserved."

"How long did you date this guy?"

"Almost a year." She spoke softly as if ashamed.

Travis couldn't keep the snarl from his lips.

"I know. I think I was just looking for someone, anyone. I was lonely. To make matters worse, I hung on until he dumped me, in public."

Another person had pushed her away. Travis placed his hand over hers and squeezed. "I'm sorry. You didn't deserve that."

"Maybe not, but that's the way it was."

He let her hand go before he held it longer than he should. "You haven't dated anyone since?"

She shook her head. "Nope, I've focused on my job. Much easier to deal with. I don't think I'm cut out for marriage and a family anyway. I've never really had a good example to follow."

"I don't know if I agree with that. We made a good team that summer."

She narrowed her eyes. "And look how that ended."

"It wasn't one of our finest moments. Let's leave it there and move on." As she placed the final tape on his arm, he lifted her chin with a finger. "It's your turn." He turned her head so he could better see her cheek. She'd already removed her bandage.

"Looks good. There may be a small scar." He picked up a plastic bandage from the table and opened it.

"It won't be the first I've had."

Her skin was too smooth and beautifully bronzed to be marred. He brushed the back of his hand over it. "It's too fine to be spoiled."

Her gaze met his and held. The air turned thick between them that had nothing to do with a fire coming their direction and everything to do with the electricity between them.

"Don't be so hard on yourself. I've been there and done that. I was supposed to have this perfect life and marriage. It didn't happen. We can't control what others do and think."

Dana looked at him. This time her eyes filled with curiosity. "That's a statement that begs for questions. What happened?" Just as quickly she said, "Hey, sorry, that's not my business."

Travis shrugged. "Water under the bridge. Let's just say while I was busy getting through medical school my wife was out partying at the clubs and going home with my classmates."

"I hate that that happened to you."

"Yeah. The worst is I took being loyal seriously and she treated it as the least important part in our marriage. Trust, partnership, working together and growing together were important to me."

"Are they still?"

"I don't know. I've not let anyone close

enough to find out. I don't do long-term relationships anymore."

"Why did your wife run around on you?" she asked, disbelief filling her voice.

Somehow that boosted his damaged ego. "She said that it was because I wasn't available. I always had to study. Or go to class. Or to the lab. I guess she was lonely."

She looked down to where she toyed with a fingernail. "I can understand that feeling. Sometimes we do stupid stuff just not to be by ourselves."

Did he carry more blame than he thought for the breakup of his marriage? That wasn't a comfortable realization. He liked it better when he'd placed all the blame on Brittney.

Dana's gaze locked with his, stayed there. She blinked. "We uh…need to finish here and get some sleep."

As sensitive as the discussion had been for both of them, at least they had broken through that glass wall between them. Those easygoing days of summer were no more. They both lugged baggage and hurt behind them that they couldn't seem to leave on the side of the road.

Dana packed away her first-aid supplies. She felt Travis's look on her but she wouldn't meet his eyes. She couldn't believe she'd just told him all that about her ex-boyfriend. She must've been tired. He'd been back in her life for less than two days and she was spilling all her secrets. Even her trail crew, who she considered her brothers, didn't know what had happened. Since Travis had shown up again it was as if she was living in a parallel universe.

And to think his wife had run around on him. Dana hoped Travis didn't think she had been taking his ex-wife's side by what she said. She believed in commitment, as well. From what she'd read between the lines, they hadn't been ready for marriage. Travis had been focused on school and his wife had been focused on herself. Dana couldn't criticize because she'd stayed with a man who ended up humiliating her. Adding to the pile of people who'd rejected her.

Travis might've hurt her feelings at one time but even then she'd admired his devotion to honesty. She stood. As she moved past him to store her kit, Travis lightly captured her wrist with a hand. She looked at him. "Yes?"

He said softly, "I've missed you. Our talks. You always had a way of making me see things differently."

"You're welcome?" She dared a look at him unsure where this would go.

"I did wonder about you. More than once."

She couldn't stop warmth from filling her. More than once he'd entered her head. Mostly as the person she judged all other men by. "Travis, I'm not that naive girl anymore. The one who had a crush on the older guy."

His gaze found hers. "I'm aware of that. I like you, Dana."

She sighed. "You shouldn't be looking at me that way."

"How am I looking at you?"

This conversation had turned a direction she hadn't expected. She took a step back. "Like I was your favorite candy."

Travis didn't move closer but her body heated as if he had. His look captured hers again. "Candy, uh? Is there something wrong with that?"

She glanced down at herself. "Yeah. I won't be your play toy. You said yourself that you don't do relationships anymore. I don't know how to do a fling."

"How do you know?"

With nervous motions she replaced her kit where it belonged. "I don't want to talk about this anymore. I think we need to keep what's between us business. That means no more personal comments or discussions."

"You sure that's want you want?" His look bored into her.

She straightened. In her firmest tone said, "I am."

"I'll agree under one condition."

"What's that?" She desperately needed him to agree.

"That I get to satisfy my curiosity."

She knew better than ask but she couldn't help herself. "About what?"

"I want to know what it would have been like to kiss you."

Her throat went dry. She shoved her hands in her pockets. "I don't think that's a good idea."

He took a half step toward her but remained out of touching distance. "Maybe not but haven't you wondered? Wouldn't you like to find out?"

Yes! No. She watched him.

"Meet me halfway, Dana," he said so softly that the roar in her ears almost kept her from hearing him.

Could she? If she didn't she'd never know. She'd wanted to kiss him then. Wanted to now. What would it hurt for them to share one kiss? She could get it out of her system. Stop wondering what it would have been like.

As she took a step forward, Travis did, as well. When they were inches apart Travis used two fingers to tip her chin up. She hardly dared to breathe. Travis Russell wanted to kiss her.

He slowly lowered his mouth.

Heat shot though her. His lips were full and firm. His first touch was gentle, tentative. She didn't back away, didn't want to. Her body trembled. She'd dreamed of this so many times. Her hands moved to his biceps, her fingers squeezing to keep from falling. Travis's hands rested on her waist steadying her. As she made a mewing sound in the back of her throat, he slanted his mouth taking the kiss deeper.

Travis pressed her more securely against him. Brushing his tongue along the seam of her mouth, asking for an invitation to enter. Dana didn't disappoint him. She wanted more. And more. This was everything she'd dreamed of, and beyond. Her mouth parted. He accepted her welcome. Wrapping her arms around Travis's neck, she clung to him.

Dana had feared she'd missed out on something special all those years ago. She had. This was what it felt like being wanted, needed.

CHAPTER FIVE

THE SQUAWK OF the radio followed by, "Come in, Dana. Come in," jerked Dana back from Travis's stupor-inducing mouth. The man could kiss. Dazed, she forced her eyes to focus and her mind to engage. She took a step toward him. She didn't want this moment to end.

They were different people now. She was stronger. Could she have some of Travis and move on?

"Dana, come in."

She pushed away but immediately missed the sizzle Travis created in her. With shaking hands, she picked up the radio. "This is Dana."

"I have an update. Fire is no longer under control. Headed your direction. Advise you move west ASAP. Over."

She felt Travis standing close behind her. "Ten-four. Will leave at first light."

"Take care. This one has turned into a monster."

"Ten-four."

She looked at Travis. "We better get some sleep. It looks like we're going to be moving fast and hard." Not waiting on a response, she went to her pack and pulled out her sleeping bag.

To her relief Travis said nothing and stepped outside. He at least was giving her time to collect herself. She needed it. The almost childish attempt at a kiss years ago came nowhere near the toe-tingling, red-hot meeting of lips they'd just shared. Travis was a master and she'd hung on for dear life. Much more and she'd be giving herself to him body and soul. Something she couldn't do.

She'd given her heart without him asking before. The hurt from his rejection still pained her. Could she live through something like that again? The bigger problem was could she resist him and live with the disappointment of not knowing what it was to kiss Travis again?

For now she had to try to settle down enough to get some rest. She'd need all her energy to make it through the next few days.

Fifteen minutes later Travis reentered the cabin. She'd already laid her sleeping bag out next to the stove. "I don't want to start a fire in the stove tonight. I don't want to have any embers left when we leave in the morning."

"Understood. You take the bed." He'd returned the mattress.

She shook her head. "I can sleep on the floor. I'm used to it."

"For heaven's sakes please let me be chivalrous for once without an argument." His tone had a bite to it.

She looked at him then. Really looked. He glared at her. "I'm sorry. I'm not used to men being chivalrous, as you put it."

He grabbed his sleeping bag from where it sat beside his equipment. "Well, you should be."

"Okay. I'll sleep on the bed. I saw a couple of extra blankets in the cabinet over there. I'll get them for you. At least you'll have some padding."

"Thank you." The early tone eased but his voice remained tight.

She dropped her sleeping bag on the bed and went after the blankets. She handed them to him. "Thanks for the bed."

"You're welcome. Good night, Dana." With that he turned his back to her, finished making his bed and climbed inside his sleeping bag.

Dana turned off the lantern. She thought of what would have been her amateur effort of kissing all those years ago and the expertise he demonstrated tonight. She shouldn't have let it go so far, but once his lips touched hers she'd been a goner. The need to kiss him, to have him kiss her had been too strong. She wouldn't let it happen again. Couldn't let it happen again.

Rejection would soon follow. She had learned the hard way it always did for her. Dana had enough of it. First her parents. Then she'd lost her grandfather. Travis, then a man she cared for. What made her think Travis would take her seriously a second time? The only reason he'd kissed her had been to settle his curiosity. He'd said so himself.

She wasn't his type, never would be. Her life was with the smokejumpers. He would want someone to hostess dinners and to go to cocktail parties. Never would she want to shame him and that would surely happen. She wouldn't be good enough for him.

She started to remove her pants.

"Leave your pants on and settle down, Dana," came Travis's husky voice. "Unless you wish me to join you. And it wouldn't be to sleep."

She held her breath not daring to move. What if she did move? Would he act on his threat? Running a finger over her bottom lip, she remembered each and every moment of

Mr. Gunter is doing." Travis walked off far enough they both could have a conversation without interrupting each other.

While still on the phone he heard a roar of a large engine. He looked up to see a low-flying tanker plane.

"Travis," Dana called with a note of urgency.

He looked to see her waving an arm for him to come. He ended his call and hurried to pick up his packs.

"We need to get out of range of these guys. The fly jockeys sometimes miss their mark. The last thing we need is to have all that fire-retardant chemical all over us."

"I couldn't agree more." Travis hustled to catch up with her.

They kept moving until they were high enough to see the sky above the trees. Dana stopped in an open area and looked back behind them. In the distance an orange-red haze hung in the air. The fire retardant floated to the ground. Farther to the north, the gray of smoke still filled the sky. The fire was still burning strong.

"What did you find out from base?" Travis asked still watching the sky.

"They're expecting a storm late afternoon and most of the night. The hope is that there's enough rain in it to help. Another electrical

Travis's kiss. It had been far better than her fumbled attempt. Maybe she should take off her pants.

No, it was better to keep things the way they were. They'd both quenched their curiosity. It was over now. Her eyes closed on an active day involving hard physical work and emotional upheaval to drift into erotic dreams starring Travis.

By the time she woke, Travis was already in the kitchen. The smell of coffee filled the air. "Breakfast in ten minutes and daylight in thirty."

His bags were already packed and waiting by the door. The few last-minute food supplies she'd left on the table where gone. He must have put them in his bags.

"You're up and ready to go."

"Let's just say I miss hot baths and a comfortable bed." He continued to work in the kitchen.

Trying to make light of the situation, she said, "At least you have goals. That'll make the walking a lot easier."

He glanced over his shoulder. "I'll keep that in mind when my feet start throbbing."

She went to the wash pan near the back door and found fresh water already in the bowl.

"Thank you." She cupped her hands together and scooped it up to splash her face. It was warm. Travis had heated water for her. She let out a loud sigh of pleasure.

"I like to hear you make that sound."

Dana looked at him to find his back still remained to her. "Thank you. That was a true gift."

He turned and smiled. "You're easy to please. And you're welcome." After placing two mugs on the table, he sat. "Let's eat."

He said that as if his ex-wife must have been difficult to please. How sad for him. Travis deserved better.

Fifteen minutes later they were ready to go. They headed out just as the sun broke over the trees. Dana took a moment to look back at the cabin. "We did all we can to save this place if the fire makes it this far."

"I'm sure Mr. Gunter will be glad we tried." Travis adjusted his pack.

They were no longer following a footpath. Dana blazed their way. Trees towered high over their heads. They spoke little as they walked. She already missed their newfound camaraderie.

Thoughts swirled through her head. Travis hadn't been exactly short with her while they ate but things had changed since they'd kissed.

She felt off center around him. As if he had shifted but she didn't know which tion.

Had she disappointed him? Was he u with her? Had she done something wrong

Travis had been following Dana for a cou of hours. All of those he'd been thinking abo their kiss. The one that had kept him up mos of the night when he'd needed sleep. He wantec to kiss her again and again. He couldn't remember when a woman had set him on fire like Dana had.

He'd had to go outside and take a few minutes to recover. Returning inside had been difficult. He'd wanted to pull her to that awful single bed and show her what they could be together. To make matters worse he was hyperaware of her soft breathing all night. Dawn came as a relief. He could get up and do something to keep his mind off Dana.

That had been working well for him until he heard her reaction to his gesture of warm water to wash with. That soft, sexy noise almost undid his good intentions.

She called a halt to their trek. "I need to check in with base."

"Okay. While you do that I'm going to try to get in touch with the hospital and see how

storm isn't what we need. It would only start more fires. How's Mr. Gunter doing?"

"Stable. He'll need a kidney transplant when they're able to move him to Seattle."

Dana briefly put her hand on his upper arm, giving him a commiserating look. "You hate not being there to see about him don't you?"

Travis's gaze met hers. Was it that transparent or did Dana understand him that well? What he did know was that his ex-wife never "got him" as Dana did. Or had he not let her? "I do. He's my patient."

"We better get going. It sounds like we're going to need to find some good shelter tonight if we don't want to get wet."

"Oh, to sleep in the rain." Travis gave one last look at the sky and turned to follow her.

"Gotten soft over the years, have you, Doc?" Her tone turned lighthearted.

"More like out of practice." Relief washed through him. At least some of the tension between them had eased. Dana hadn't met his eyes all morning. He'd convinced himself he'd been wrong to ask to kiss her. He should've known better. Somehow in a weak moment he'd thought if they did, it might clear the air some. All it had done was make it thicker. He'd had no idea it would be so explosive.

"I bet it'll come back to you." The words were thrown over her shoulder

An hour of hard walking later, they reached a peak.

"We'll rest here." Dana dropped her packs and sank to the ground, her legs crossed.

Travis joined her, leaning his back against a boulder. "Where are we?"

"To the west of Skeleton Cave Trail. We may need to turn south some. The going's harder there but we have a better chance of finding some protection from the weather."

Travis dug into his personal pack and pulled out two granola bars. He offered her one. "Sounds like a must-see."

Dana laughed and took the bar. "Some of these trails were named ages ago."

Hearing her laugh was like having the sun come up just for him.

"Goodness, if I'd realized a snack bar would be that appreciated I would've given you one earlier."

"I might not have been as happy to receive it then as I am now."

He chuckled. "Point taken." Looking up at the beauty around them, he recognized that Dana belonged here. She'd be swallowed up, and shrivel up in an office building. Her world was in nature. Had her ex-boyfriend not seen that? Or had he not cared?

Dana had a wildness to her, an untamed quality that called to him. He didn't want to master it, just taste it and be carried along with it. That sense of who she was only added to her beauty. Her draw. His need.

"You're staring at me again." She took a bite of her bar. "This is the third time."

His look didn't leave her. "I'm sorry. I tend to do that when I'm fascinated by someone."

Pink that had nothing to do with the effort of walking came to her cheeks. That only charmed him more. As tough as Dana acted, she could still blush.

"What's that supposed to mean? Fascination."

He took another bite out of his bar as he continued to watch her. "Being interested or amazed by something."

Her lips tightened as she gave him a disgusted look. "I know the definition of fascination. I'm just wondering why you'd be fascinated by me."

"Why wouldn't I be? The fact that you can outwork most people I know. You jump out of airplanes. You're so feminine yet you work in a man's world. You've the most luscious lips.

And you can kiss like there's no tomorrow. Need I go on?"

There was a long pause where only the sounds of birds and the rustle of the wind could be heard.

"Why're you sweet-talking me? I'm not what you want. I told you I'm not going to be your play thing."

"I'm not trying to sweet-talk you. You asked me a question and I answered it. Honestly. Whether you believe that or not is up to you."

She looked toward the forest. "What I think is you're dumping a load of bear scat at my feet."

That hurt. He'd meant every word he'd said. Had she heard so few compliments in her life she couldn't believe one when it was given? "Why would you say that? Not everyone is as ignorant as the men you've apparently been out with. You ex-boyfriend being a prime example. Just because you haven't been out with a good guy doesn't mean they don't exist."

She shifted to hold more of her back to him. Dana wasn't comfortable with this discussion but he wasn't gonna let her off the hook. She needed to know how desirable and interesting she was. To know that her kisses could turn his insides into hot liquid.

"Is this part of that bedside manner that's

required to be a doctor?" She stuffed her trash into her pocket.

"How like you to put a man in his place. I can see that sweet-talking you isn't your thing. Maybe I need to try my caveman technique."

She twisted to glare at him. "Don't you dare! I have a chain saw and know how to use it."

Travis leaned back and roared with a laughter. The birds flew out of the trees and small animals hurried to their holes. It was the first real laugh he'd had in a long time. It felt good.

"I think it's time we get moving." She stood and gathered her things including the chain saw.

To her back he said, "Just because you don't want to believe something doesn't make it not be true."

Finally the ground leveled off enough he could walk beside her. A loud screech came from the sky. He looked up to see an eagle, wings spread wide soaring overhead. "This truly is amazing country, isn't it?"

"It is." Dana's voice held a sound of awe. "But for all its beautiful, wild, breathtaking elements it can be deadly, as well."

Too soon they reentered the woods and started downhill. At one particularly steep spot they had to hold tree saplings to keep themselves upright. When Dana slid to her side Travis grabbed the chain saw before it and she went tumbling. Bracing himself against a tree in order not to go down, he helped her to right herself.

Dana worked farther along, still using the trees as support until she could stand by leaning back against a tree. She reached for the chain saw. Travis handed it down then climbed past her. They followed the leapfrog pattern until they were on flatter ground.

He stopped beside Dana. "You okay?"

She shrugged and wiped her hands on her pants. "Scraped my hands but no big deal. I should be wearing my gloves."

"Let me see." He took her hands and lifted them. Both had small red marks across them.

Before he realized what he was doing he kissed one palm then the other.

"Travis…" His name was little more than a whisper across her lips.

He picked up the chain saw and started off. "Let me lead for a while." To his astonishment she didn't argue. She must have been as shocked as he that he'd kissed her hands.

Dana watched Travis's back. What had that been about? Whatever it was, he left her heart fluttering in her chest. She'd had such a crush on Travis once. Was it so hard to believe that she could again? Would it be so terrible if she did? The thought took a firmer hold the more she was around him. She hurried to catch him.

The roar of water rushing over rocks grew stronger. Travis stood beside a creek by the time she joined him.

"Should we cross here or is there a better spot?"

Dana looked across the rocky area. "This is as good a place as any. It's miles downstream before the stream calms."

"We cross here then." Travis picked up the saw by the handle.

"Go slow. The goal here is not only to cross but to stay dry. We can't build a fire this time of the year to dry things out."

"I'll keep that in mind." Travis took a wide step putting a foot on a rock with water washing around it. Using the saw as a counterbalance, he moved farther into the stream.

When he had made it halfway across, she followed using his path. They made slow progress but wearing wet clothes all day wouldn't be fun. She concentrated on each movement of her feet. Glancing over, she saw Travis had made it to the other side. He placed the saw and his bags on the ground.

She returned her attention to what she was doing. The next step had undoubtedly been easy for Travis but was wider than she felt comfortable making. Looking around for an alternative rock, she couldn't find one.

"Stay put." Travis called. "I'm coming after you."

Before she could stay anything, he'd already left the bank.

"Give me your hand." She did and his strong one closed around hers. "Step over here to me. This rock is large enough to hold us both."

When she teetered, his grip tightened, holding her in place before his hands came to her waist. They stood chest to chest as water rushed around them. She didn't dare look him in the eyes for fear she'd forget they were in the center of the creek.

"The last step is wide also. I'm going to step across and swing you over. Don't move until I have firm footing." She did as he said. "On three." His words brushed her ear. He lifted her with ease and soon her feet were on dry ground.

As she moved away to give him room to join her, he stepped to the bank but lost his footing when part of the bank gave way. Dana grabbed his hand and pulled. She fell to the ground hard, her breath leaving her with an *oof.* Travis came down on top of her. They were in a tangle of arms and legs. She worked to catch her breath.

"Dana, are you all right? Did I hurt you?" Panic filled Travis's voice as he scrambled off her.

Pulling in enough air to speak, she said, "I'm okay."

"You sure?" Concern darkened his eyes.

"I'm fine."

Travis stood and reached out a hand and helped her stand. He studied her. "Are you sure you aren't hurt?"

"I'm good. Really." Her voice held a gruffness. Was it from the fall or having Travis so near? She adjusted her packs. "We need to keep moving."

He picked up his belongings. "You're sure I didn't hurt you. You took a hard fall especially with my weight crushing you."

"Travis, I said I'm fine. Now let's go." Why couldn't he leave it alone? She wasn't used to having someone show concern for her. Guilt ate at her. She should appreciate his worry. They hadn't hiked far when she turned to him. "I'm sorry I made a fuss about you making sure I was all right. I've spent years trying to be tough enough to handle my job. Showing any weakness might affect my performance. I'm sensitive about it."

"You're human. You can hurt. Can show it." Had all her life been spent proving herself worthy?

She looked away. "I know. But I don't like to show it."

"Hey." He waited until her gaze returned to him. "You can let it show with me. I promise to have your back."

"Thanks. That's nice to hear." She looked at the sky. It had filled with ominous low dark clouds. "We need to start looking for shelter. One of the guys I used to work with out of Bend told me about a small cave in this area. We're going to look for it."

"Is that with or without a bear?"

Dana grinned. "We're going to plan for without."

"Good. I've almost met my quota for an eventful day."

"I have to admit this trip gets more interesting all the time. It sure would make a nice end to the day if we could find that cave."

Travis slapped the side of his leg. "Then let's go do it."

CHAPTER SIX

TRAVIS TRAILED BEHIND DANA up and over the rocks. She didn't seem to give up and acted as if nothing was too tough for her. He'd gotten so used to being around hothouse, needy women he'd forgotten what a truly capable woman acted like. The only issue he had with that was she worked at it too hard. As if she always had to prove herself.

With sure feet, she continued up the mountain, half pulling herself along. He made every step she did while searching the area for a cave opening. The chain saw shifted on his shoulder. Though it was cumbersome but necessary, he still wished he could leave it behind. But that wouldn't happen. They might need it. He moved it to the other shoulder. Still a guy could dream…

They maneuvered through a narrow space between two rocks on their upward climb. Every once in a while Dana stopped and searched the outcroppings. They marched on as dark clouds continued to roll in and shut out the sunlight, lightning flashes within them. The air thickened. The storm now hung low over the distant tree line. It would be an angry one.

"Hey, Travis."

"Yeah."

"Tell me about your ex-wife."

That came out of the blue. "What do you want to know?"

"Whatever you'll tell me." Dana made it sound as if they were having a casual conversation to pass the time.

"She is tall, has blond hair and likes the finer things in life."

Dana asked over her shoulder, "Did your parents like her?"

He climbed over a rock. "I guess so."

"Did you love her?"

Had he? Really? "I think I thought she'd be the perfect partner for the life I had envisioned. I met her in college. She'd been raised as a princess so she knew all the social ins and outs. I thought I needed that to get ahead in my profession. She dressed like a fashion plate. Wanted the house to look just so. But none of that really has anything to do with love, does it?"

Dana stopped and looked back at him. "No."

How misguided he'd been. He'd not only done Brittney an injustice but himself, as well. He'd been so wrapped up in creating the perfect picture, he produced a nightmare. Moments later Dana's excited call had him hurrying forward.

"I think I've found it." She pointed above them. "Stay here and I'll check it out."

"Dana, let me go."

With a flashlight already out, she looked at him. "I've got this. You don't have to take care of me."

"I know that, but you could let someone do it every once in a while. I've the caring gene. Remember? I'm a doctor."

She'd already started up the side of the mountain. "I'll keep that in mind."

"Watch out for a bear," he yelled.

"Will do. I promise if one's in there you'll know it almost as soon as I do."

Fear shot through him. Travis dropped the chain saw to a nearby rock. "You don't think…"

"Calm down. I think if there's one it would've shown up by now." She kept moving. Closer to the black hole she slowed. Turning on the flashlight, she crawled nearer the opening.

When he could no longer see her Travis held

his breath, his muscles tensed. If there was a bear and Dana got hurt, could he get her to help fast enough? He didn't even want to think about the possibilities.

He released the breath he'd held as she backed out of the hole. "I'm fine. It'll hold both of us, but just barely. At least it'll block the majority of the rain." All of her disappeared briefly again before she back out and called, "All clear. Home sweet home. For the night."

Travis carried all the supplies he could up and handed them to her. While she took them inside he returned for the rest.

Dana had already stored what she could at the back of the cave and had their sleeping bags spread out.

"Hurry up and settle in. The show is about to begin."

He couldn't miss the delight in her voice. "Show?"

"The light show." She pointed toward the sky.

A flash of lightning in the middle of the black cloud at eye level was nothing like he'd ever seen. He sat on his sleeping bag, hunched over because he couldn't sit straight.

Dana turned around and lay on her stomach propping her chin on her folded hands like a kid watching her favorite cartoon. He followed her example.

As he relaxed, she handed him two packages of MREs. "If you eat all your meat and vegetables then you can have dessert."

He wished that included her but he wouldn't push. Anything further would be up to her to suggest.

Thunder rolled, clouds thickened making it more difficult to see. Lightning flashed, and a second later the next flash came. He grinned at her. "I get it now. Dinner and a show. Dana, you do know how to show a man a good time."

She opened one of her bags. "What can I say? The vantage point can't be beat."

They ate in silence. It would've been hard to talk over the noise of the storm anyway. The tempest slowly worked its way toward him. The first fat drop of rain fell in front of them and quickly turned into a deluge. The air drew damp.

They watched for almost an hour before the rain turned steady. "I think this might be one of the most amazing things I've ever seen."

"It never grows old. My grandfather used to say the gods were arguing."

"That's a nice way to think about it."

"It's an amazing show of nature but it can be rough on the people below."

Even in the dim light he could see the sadness in her eyes. "That sounds like you have some experience with that."

Dana didn't say anything for a while. "My grandfather's barn caught fire. He'd run inside to save the cow and horse. They made it out but a timber fell on him. For the rest of his life he walked with a limp and had horrible scars. I learned to respect the weather."

"The hard way I'd say."

"Why did you live with your grandfather?" He'd never asked that summer and she'd never said. He wanted to know more about Dana. Understand her.

"My parents left me with him when I was five. Time for me to start school. See, my parents were wannabe musicians. They left me with Grandpa to go on the road. They were in a bus accident and killed when I was eight."

"I'm sorry."

"It's no big deal. I think I was an accident anyway. They didn't need a kid hanging around. I didn't see them but once or twice a year and only for a day or so. I didn't really know them."

"Hey, they're the ones who missed out." Travis placed a hand on her back, gently rubbed it. She had more than her share of loss in her life. He couldn't imagine not having his par-

ents to help support him when times were bad.
They'd certainly been there for him when he'd
gotten a divorce. Even if they weren't together,
they still cared about him.

"That's a nice thing to say."

Another flash of lightning let him clearly
see her face. It was angelic. The talk of her
parents hadn't taken away from her enjoyment
of the moment. She understood the majesty
of the world she worked in and her place in it.
Could he say as much about himself? What a
nice place to be in life. "Thanks for sharing
the show with me. I'll remember it always."

She smiled. "You are welcome."

"In many ways this has been an amazing
trip."

"I'm going to get some sleep on that thought.
Good night." She turned around, opened her
sleeping bag and slipped inside. "See you in
the morning." Dana positioned her personal
bag as a pillow, then removed her pants and
placed them nearby. She rolled to her side putting her back to him.

Just like that she forgot about him. For some
reason he didn't like the idea. Why it bothered him he didn't know. He wanted her as
flustered by him being near as he was by her
being so close.

Everything about Dana spoke of home, family, forever. He'd tried that and it hadn't gone well. He wasn't interested in taking a chance again. Didn't trust his judgement. His discussion with Dana about love had proved he didn't understand that feeling. Still he didn't like Dana not noticing he was alive.

Last night he'd believed she did, especially when he kissed her. She responded. Acted as if she enjoyed it. Wanted more. But he'd misread women before. He'd certainly thought his ex-wife had been something she wasn't. Could he be doing the same with Dana?

Since Dana had settled in for the night it was more difficult for him to maneuver. Trying not to disturb her, he worked himself into his bag and out of his pants. His body would stay warmer by putting on clothes in the morning.

Clasping his hands behind his head as a pillow, he listened to the rain. His mind returned to Dana who lay so close. Thankfully he was exhausted and soon drifted off to sleep.

A moan and the chatter of teeth woke him. Dana had shifted beside him and now curled into him. Still she shivered. The temperature had dropped after the storm.

He unzipped his bag and then hers, pulling her against his body. She lay on her side turned into him. Her nose snuggled into his neck. A hand came to lie across his chest and a leg wrapped one of his, her feet nestled with his. Working slowly and carefully, he managed to get her bag over them and tucked around her.

Placing an arm around her waist, he pulled her closer, if that was possible. With a sigh and warmth circling in his chest, he fell back to sleep.

The next time he woke the palm of her hand circled his middle and a soft moan brushed his neck. His manhood instantly came to attention. Feet rubbed against his, then cool toes were stuffed beneath his calf. The hand stopped over his heart. Dana stilled. He drifted off again.

The shove of a hand on his chest and a knee in the side of his thigh brought him awake. He grunted and opened his eyes to see snapping eyes glaring down at him.

"What're you doing in my sleeping bag?" Dana demanded.

Raising a brow, he kept his tone even. "You're in mine."

She blinked, then looked down at their combined bodies as if to confirm his statement. "How?"

"You were cold. Shivering. You crawled over to me. You sure do have cold toes."

She jerked them out from under his calf. "We better get up and get moving."

"It's not light enough yet. Calm down. I'm

not going to attack you. Close your eyes and enjoy listening to the world come alive."

Dana eased down but remained tense beside him.

He squeezed her waist slightly. "Stop thinking. Just be for a change."

It took a few minutes but Dana relaxed against him. Her breathing even. She'd gone to sleep. They stayed like that until he could easily see the area outside. He gave Dana a gentle shake. "It's light."

Her lips brushed his neck.

He went motionless. "Dana?"

That touch found the curve between his neck and shoulder. "Mmm…"

Her hips moved along his.

She couldn't possibly know what she was doing. "Dana. We need to get up."

"I'd rather stay here." She nestled against him.

"Sweetheart, I sure as hell want to, but we're not going to. I won't have you regretting anything that happens between us ever again. This isn't the time or the place." He reached across her and picked up Dana's pants. He laid them on top of her.

He pushed the bag off him, picked up his pants and pulled them on, trying not to think about the warm, desirable Dana so nearby.

Had he lost his mind? Sexual attraction had hummed like a live electrical wire between them since her boss's office. When they came together he wanted them to have more than a hurried meeting in a tiny cave in the middle of nowhere. He needed to know Dana wanted it, as well. Give her time to think. Not take her in the heat of the moment.

He dared a glance at her. She had dressed. Together they worked to pack up their supplies. They were ready to leave when he took Dana's hand.

"What?" she said not looking at him, as she tugged on her hand.

Travis held it and led her out of the cave to where they could stand up. Brushing a strand of hair back from her face, he waited until she'd looked at him. He gave her a light kiss on the lips. "I don't know for sure what's going though that head of yours right now but I've a pretty good idea. So I want to make it perfectly clear that when I have a chance I'm going to kiss you, all over. Don't doubt for a minute that I want you."

Dana had no idea what to say so she said nothing. She couldn't believe her own actions. What had she done? She'd been keeping Travis at arm's length for days and this morning she woke to his heat and lost her mind. She spent the entire day before thinking about kissing him again, wanting him. Snuggled against Travis, she couldn't resist acting on her desire.

This trip would be a short amount of time so why shouldn't she enjoy Travis while it lasted? Their summer together was temporary, this trip would be, as well. But with a better ending. They'd return to civilization and life would go back to normal. They'd enjoy each other for a while, then have nice memories and move on.

She watched Travis for a moment as he led the way down to the path. Her chest filled with the hope of what would come. Travis hadn't said no. Instead he was postponing. He wanted her. He hadn't rejected her. Instead he promised her soon. That's what she needed to remember.

On the path she said, "I need to check in. It'll determine which way we go."

"Okay. I'll do the same." He shrugged off his large bag and fished out his phone before he stepped away.

A couple of minutes later Travis rejoined her.

"What's the word?" He took out his water bottle and drank.

"The good news is the rain put the majority

of the fire out. Bad news, we still have a long walk out. How's Mr. Gunter doing?"

"The same. They're preparing to transfer him today or tomorrow." Travis picked up his bag. "What's our plan?"

"We're headed for the tower off Bessie Butte Trail. We'll stay there tonight. If all goes well we'll hike out tomorrow and someone can pick us up."

Travis nodded. "Good deal. That sounds promising."

"The downside is we've got a ten-mile hike today." She started along the trail.

What she didn't say was she hoped they could remain on the path for as long as possible. They'd soon have to get off and create their own again which would make the going harder and slower. If weather deterred them they'd be in further trouble. Being responsible for Travis added to her concern. Yet they had to push on if they wanted to make the tower by nightfall.

"We can't stop to eat today. Sorry."

"Okay." He pulled two bags of MREs out of the lower side pocket of his pants. He handed one to her. "Enjoy."

Travis didn't complain—she'd give him that. Dana took the package. She ate as she walked. Grabbing a limb to steady herself, she descended another rocky path. Over the next hour they concentrated on climbing down the mountain. They hiked out into a wide-open meadow with a stream flowing through it. Mountains created a beautiful clearing. Birds flew up in front of them as they walked.

"I have to admit I've enjoyed seeing a part of the country I've never visited. The beauty is amazing." Travis moved up to stroll beside her. "I forgot what it was to walk for days to get home after fighting a fire."

"I always find it ironic when we jump in and fight a fire for half a day then have to walk two days to get out."

"Isn't that still a score of pride for the smokejumpers? They walk out when the hotshots ride."

"Yeah. They're *much* weaker," Dana said proudly.

"You never told me why you wanted to be a smokejumper. It's an unusual job for a woman."

"That's pretty easy. My fifth-grade class went on a field trip to the base station. I thought it was the most amazing place I'd ever been. A couple of jumpers talked to us. Let us put on equipment. We even climbed in a plane. I decided that day I wanted to be a smokejumper.

When my grandfather got hurt it sealed the deal."

"And you never looked back."

"And I never looked back. I wanted to be the best of the best." Complete confidence surrounded her words. "To do something that really mattered."

"There're less dangerous ways to do that."

"Sure there are, but I found a home with the smokejumpers. It took some major work on my part to prove myself but I have." She'd worked out more, studied harder and done jobs no one else wanted. Had proven herself worthy. Found a place where she was valued and wouldn't be pushed out. A place where she was wanted and needed.

"From what I can tell all that paid off."

Her chin rose with pride. Travis sounded as if he admired her. "Thanks for saying that. I like to think so. High praise since this trip has been such a fiasco. I thought it would be more straightforward but that's part of the charm of the job. You never know what's going to happen. How about you? Did you feel the same about medicine?"

"I did, and do. All it took for me to know I'd found my place was the look on an older gentleman's face when I told him he would be fine and could go home to his wife of fifty-five years. I just wish all my decisions had been as clear and correct."

"We all make mistakes. It's what we learn from them and do about them that matters."

Travis made a sound of agreement. "That's a deep bit of wisdom. Have you managed to follow it?"

"I've tried but haven't always been success-ful. I'm still working on it."

Travis looked at Dana's profile as they con-tinued across the wide meadow. Why did she seem to have it all together while he was still fumbling with life? "Why didn't we ever talk about this before?"

Back during their summer together had he just been in his own world? Concerned only with what he planned for his life. It was just as well he hadn't let their relationship go beyond that almost kiss. He hadn't deserved Dana. Didn't like the man he'd become since then as well. They had both changed. Her for the better. Him not so much.

"I don't know. We were focused on training and having fun during our down hours. To talk about our dreams and plans maybe had been too serious."

Back then he'd had his entire life mapped out, yet most of it hadn't turned out as expected. He'd given up on plans and hopes. Now he just lived, took what came.

"There's supposed to be a footbridge along here somewhere."

Dana's statement drew him out of his musings. He looked around. They'd arrived at a wide stream.

"Since it's the dry season the water is low. If it were spring this water would be high and rushing. We'd have no chance of crossing without getting wet." She looked up and down the creek. "If we don't find the bridge it'll add an hour to our walk."

"You do love a challenge."

She strolled ahead. "There has to be some way across. There." She pointed ahead. "It narrows." Hurrying forward she called, "And look! A log."

"You've got to be kidding. A log isn't a bridge. You really expect us to cross on that?"

She grinned back at him. "I thought you liked a challenge." Picking up a stick, Dana returned to the log. "Didn't you say you wanted to work on your tightwire act?"

"No. And if I did I'd rather not start with a log lying across a cold creek in the middle of nowhere when I can't build a fire."

"Afraid to live dangerously, are you, Doc?" Dana placed a foot on the log to test it. Bounced it a few times. "It seemed sturdy enough. Look at it this way. If you go in it's only a couple of more miles to the tower where there's a propane heater. And if your boots get wet you only have one more day to walk in them."

He stood on the bank watching her. "That's all supposed to make me feel better?"

"I'll talk to you on the other side. You're distracting me." Dana stuck the stick into the water using it to help balance as she moved farther out on the log.

She'd been distracting him for days and she expected him to feel sorry for her. "At least that's a positive. For a while there I wasn't sure you knew I was alive."

She glanced back. "Oh, I knew you were alive. That was the problem. Now hush and let me concentrate." She shifted her foot out another step.

With the next one, Dana rocked back and almost lost her footing. He sucked in a breath. She wasn't going to make it. He dropped his packs and the chain saw. If he had to go in he didn't want anything extra hanging on him.

Dana continued moving out over the water.

A crack of sound barely reached his ears before the snap of the log breaking echoed across the prairie. Dana yelped, falling in the water backward. If the situation hadn't been dire, the look of surprise on her face would've been comical. Instead she went under. The weight of the pack on her back holding her down.

Travis didn't hesitate to jump in. By the time he managed to get to Dana she'd rolled over but still fought to get her feet under her. He grabbed her around the waist. "Stop struggling. I've got you."

Dana relaxed.

They continued to float down the river.

"We're going to slowly make our way over to the bank." They kicked and paddled in unison without Travis letting her go toward the grassy edge. There he pushed Dana with a hand to her bottom while she pulled herself upward until she lay on her stomach. With what energy he had left, he grabbed a handful of grass and tugged his way out of the water beside her. They both lay there heaving.

"Are you okay?" Travis asked fearing she'd hit her head or worse while struggling.

"Yeah. But now we're both wet." She sounded disgusted.

"Should I have just let you drown?" He sat up.

"No. I do appreciate you helping me. The pack weighted me down and falling backward made it worse."

"We still have to cross over." Travis rolled

to his knees and hands, then stood. He took her by the elbows and helped her stand. "This time it won't matter if we get wet or not. This time I think I'll be the outside boss and we'll try it my way."

Dana's hands went to her hips. "Which'll be?"

"Find a shallow place to cross. Our feet are already wet. Let's go pick up my stuff and see how fast we can get to some place where we can take off these wet clothes."

They walked back up the bank. Travis picked up his supplies and they kept moving. The river remained wide for a way but he soon found a rocky area.

"This should do it." He looked at her. "We'll go across together this time. Take my hand."

She gave him an indignant look, crossing her arms over her chest. "I can handle myself."

"Why do you always have to be so independent?" He pumped his hand offering it again. "It's not a sin to accept help."

"Maybe it's because I've always had to take care of myself."

His look met hers. "Then this time let me help take care of you. Grab my hand. I promise not to let you go."

Her gaze locked with his. Her eyes flickered

with surprise, questions and possibly hope. Slowly she placed her hand in his.

Something significant had happened but he wasn't sure what. He stepped into the water. "I won't let you fall."

Her gaze met his. "I know you won't."

Travis got the idea her words meant more than the obvious as if she were giving him a vote of confidence she hadn't given another man. He didn't wish to disappoint her.

Dana joined him in the water and they slowly worked their way across. When her foot slipped he held her hand tightly and placed a hand at her underarm steadying her. They looked at each other. He would've kissed her if they hadn't been standing in the middle of a river. "We need to keep moving. We're almost there."

She nodded.

At the bank, he climbed out then helped her.

Dana removed her big pack and set the saw down. "Time to empty our boots."

"Now? Can't we do that when we get to the tower?"

"I recommend you don't wait. Take them off and dump out as much water as possible. Also ring out your socks. You don't want your feet to get unhappy."

"I'll be okay."

She put her hand on his arm. "I promise you won't be if you don't do as I say."

Travis took a seat on the ground beside her. "It's hard for me to believe my feet could be any more uncomfortable than they already are."

"You get foot rot and you'll find out different." She pulled off one of her boots and turned it upside down.

He did the same and water tricked out.

"Hand me the shirt slash towel." He dug through his pack and found it. She picked up one of his feet.

"What're you doing?"

She dried his foot making sure to get between the toes.

"Hey, that tickles." He pulled back on his foot.

She hung on. "I can't take a chance you don't get them dry as possible. I'm responsible for getting you back in one piece." She put that one down and started on the other. "We'll dry everything out the best we can tonight. By the way, thanks for saving me."

"You're welcome."

"I hope you brought a change of socks." She put his foot down.

Travis patted his bag. "Right here."

"Good. It'll be important you wear them to-morrow."

He shifted so that he could dry Dana's feet, placing one on his thigh. She had such a trim ankle. "If I didn't know better I'd think this was some erotic foreplay."

Her cheeks pinked. She lowered her head. "You'd think that until the skin started peeling off."

"I've seen trench foot. It's not very attractive." Travis had never been a foot guy but he liked Dana's. They were long and narrow. To his surprise her toes were polished a bright pink. "Hot pink, uh?"

Those rosy spots on her cheek grew.

He continued to dry her foot giving each toe special attention. Finished with that one, he picked up the other. Taking more time than required, he gave it the same devotion.

Dana cleared her throat. "We should be going." She picked up one of her socks and rung it out, ready to put it on.

"Don't." Travis reached inside his pack and pulled out a plastic bag. He removed a pair of socks and handed them to her.

"I can't take your socks. You won't have any dry ones."

He dug around in his bag again and pulled out a bag. "I have another pair."

"What're you, a Boy Scout?"

He raised his chin and gave her a cheeky grin. "No. I've just learned from experience to be prepared."

"You'd think I'd know better." She accepted the socks from him.

"I know you do just fine on your own but every once in a while we all need help." He suddenly wished she did need him. But could he be that guy?

"Look who's dishing out wisdom now."

With their socks and boots back on, Travis helped Dana with her pack and picked up his bags. "Which way, oh, great leader?"

"Are you relinquishing the bossing duty to me again?" She grinned.

"I am?"

"As it should be."

He gave a loud huff.

She smiled and pointed off to the north. "See that second peak over there?"

"Yeah."

"Can you make out that tiny dot above it in the sky?"

"Yep." He stood beside her.

"That's the top of the fire tower and our destination tonight. Do you think you have it in you to make it?" Her eyes held a dare.

Travis pushed his chin out. "I'll try not to hold you back."

She smiled. "I'll let you know if you do."

Travis nudged her with an elbow. "I've no doubt you'll point it out when I do."

They started across the flat plain with the knee-high grass wrapping their legs so dry bits of shaft blew in the wind around them. An hour later they reached the tree line and started their climb.

"Talk to me, Dana. Tell me about your ranch. How big is it?"

"You really want to know about that?" she asked over her shoulder.

"I do." He wanted to know all he could about her.

Dana wasn't sure how much of her life she wanted to share with him. But if she answered his questions then she had the right to ask some of her own.

"I have almost ten acres just south of Redmond with a small house and barn." It was her heaven when she wasn't working. "It needed a lot of work when I inherited it. I've spent most of my time redoing it." She wove through the trees. Thankfully the space between the wide, tall trees made it easier to walk.

"Does the house have a porch?" Travis asked from close behind her.

Why had he asked such a specific question? "It does. A large one across the front with a swing."

"From the sound of your voice you clearly love the place."

"I do. It's my home." It belonged to her and couldn't be taken away. Wouldn't leave her.

"Sounds much nicer than my condo with the thin walls. Any animals?"

Travis really was curious. "I board a few horses for a friend. Have two barn cats."

She thought to invite him for a visit but stopped herself. What they had would end when they returned to town. She didn't expect more. She couldn't count on it being different.

They came to a dense stand of timber where the ground was covered with moss and ferns. Dana took a seat on a fallen log. "Let's rest."

"I didn't know you could." Travis sat beside her. "Down here it's hard to believe it can burn."

Dana looked up to where the dappled light came through the trees. "The tops of the trees are often not so lucky. All it takes is a lightning strike and they go up."

"Still here it looks like elves should be jumping out at us."

His words said he missed little in his observations. That no doubt made him a good doctor. What did he see in her? She chuckled. "I had no idea you had such an imagination."

"Hang out with me and you might learn a lot more things. How're your feet doing?" Travis stretched out his legs.

"Pretty good. What about yours?"

Concern filled his eyes as he looked down at her. "They've been better. But I have to admit dry socks were nice. For a while."

"We should get going. We're losing daylight. I'd rather not climb the staircase of the fire tower in the dark."

Travis stood and offered her his hand. She placed hers in it. So strong and warm. Secure. Her problem when they returned to their own world wouldn't be having taken his help but with letting it go. Yet she had to. They weren't meant to be. The only reason he was still here was because he had no choice. Otherwise he'd have been long gone.

They walked for another thirty minutes before they came to an opening where they could see the valley and the river they'd just crossed.

Travis took her hand. "This has to be the most spectacular view. Just gorgeous. This extra hike might not have been our choice but I'm glad I get to share this with you."

She looked at him instead of the view. A honeyed feeling filled her middle making it flutter. Heaven help her, Travis had started to get to her. She wanted a little of what might have been.

CHAPTER SEVEN

Travis followed Dana's lead and kept the pace. They had started downhill again. Thankfully it was more of a meandering walk then before. Soon they were starting back up again.

"When we reach the top we only have a little ways to go before we get to the fire tower."

Sweat ran down the center of his back. His overgrown facial hair itched. Every once in a while he tugged on his damp pants, pulling them away from where they stuck to his legs. His pack grew heavier with each step. He could imagine Dana felt much the same discomfort. Since her bags were wet they must weigh more yet she didn't slow or let him carry them.

Finally they reached a rise and he could see the fire tower clearly. Without breaking her pace, Dana continued along the winding path to the top of the mountain.

The sun lowered. Light had become limited.

What started out as a medical mission to help a deathly ill patient had turned into brutal days of hiking. Dana hadn't uttered a single complaint and he didn't intend to either. Despite the fact that his feet were killing him and he'd worked up a blister that hurt like the devil.

"How much farther?"

"Hour. Maybe a little more."

He took another step forward.

Dana looked up. "We're either going to have to push through or make camp."

"This close I say we push through." He wanted comfort and shelter. He had no interest in staying out in weather like last night's.

"Agreed."

Was Dana as determined in every area of her life? He suspected she was. He looked forward to getting caught up in that determination when he had her in his arms. And he'd have her there soon, especially after what happened this morning. He had been shocked at her clear want of him, but he would willingly accept it. Desperately wanted her. He would make the most of the time they had together. Even if he could only offer her now and no more. His heart would remain firmly behind a closed door.

Sooner than he'd expected, they reached a

small building constructed on a metal frame that stood six stories high.

Travis had never been so glad to see something in his life. He'd seen pictures of fire towers but had never been up in one. Dark was almost on them. He was tired, hungry and damp and had had enough walking. They crossed the middle of the field.

He put his foot on the first iron rung of the stairs. It consisted of six steps then a platform and six more steps until it reached the top. Looking up, he considered the climb. "Do we stop for a rest or do we keep moving?"

"I'm afraid if I stop I won't get started again. The only downside to that idea is the outhouse is all the way down here." Dana glanced at the small building sitting thirty feet away.

"Both are good points."

"Outhouse later. Wet clothes first." He pulled himself up the first step. "I had no idea these were still being used."

"Mostly they're not for their original purpose. Many are not tall enough to see as large an area as necessary. And technology has gotten so much better they have become obsolete. We have so many better ways of detection now. Mostly they're used by hikers or tourists as a place to stay."

"A rustic hotel room." He'd take any place with a roof and some semblance of relief.

"Yeah, something like that. I'm glad to see no one's rented this one tonight." Dana's booted steps sounded behind him.

"They would've had to share." Travis looked up to find they were only halfway to the top. "We'd have asked nicely."

"Whatever way we did it, we at least have shelter for tonight and a chance to have some heat."

He looked at her. "There's never-ending fun with you."

"Thanks, I think. Don't tell me you're tired of walking in wet shoes."

"I've had enough for the day, the week and possibly the month."

Dana chuckled. "If you need any encouragement there should be a cold shower, canned food and a not-very-good bed. But it'll offer a breathtaking view."

"I'm moving on." He took another step.

"Oh, one more selling point. We won't get wet if it rains."

"All the comforts of home." Travis grinned. He liked the banter between them. It was nice they had found this in their relationship. He hoped there was more of it to come. "Based on the sky, it doesn't look like that's gonna be a problem tonight."

They were almost to the top.

Travis took the landing and started up the last six steps. Above his head was the catwalk that circled the twelve-by-twelve room, glass on all four sides. He climbed through the hole and kept moving until he stood on the catwalk waiting for Dana.

She joined him, then went to the door in the middle of the wall. Turning the knob, she grinned at him when it opened. She pushed it wide and stepped inside.

He followed. "Looks like home sweet home."

Dana chuckled low in her throat. "I think that might be an exaggeration but I'll certainly take it."

The entire building was smaller than his bedroom at the condo. In one corner was a counter, a stove with two burners, and a mini refrigerator. A table with two chairs sat nearby. In the opposite corner stood a bed of sorts made out of wood with an "iffy" mattress, but space enough for two people. In another area were two small, cushioned chairs with a shelf full of books. Simple, and everything they needed to survive.

In the middle of the room stood a round fixture, waist high on him, that had an eighteen-inch map on it.

"What's this?" he ran his hand over the top of the clear covering.

"It's an Osborne Firefinder. It is used to locate the position of a fire. The lookout would then radio in the coordinates. Each tower has one. Old-school stuff now."

"Yeah, but there was some artistry to the old-fashioned way." He continued to study the apparatus.

"Why, Dr. Russell, you continue to surprise me. You can appreciate the simpler times. I always liked the idea of the lone man waiting and watching for that puff of smoke and calling it in."

"The alone part would take a special person. I'm not sure I could be here days upon end by myself." He put his pack down. Unless he had her with him. Wow, where had that idea come from?

Dana unload her bags. "I've gotten used to being by myself so I don't think I'd mind. Enough of that. We need to get busy before it turns dark. I'll check on the propane. Why don't you check on the rain barrel?"

Travis headed out the door and around the catwalk. He located the shower that was much like Mr. Gunter's. He returned inside. "Plenty of water. My guess courtesy of the storm last night."

"Good. We've enough propane too. I found a few canned goods that were left behind. Renters are supposed to take everything with them but some leave their extras behind for people like us. We'll use it because I want to save anything we have in case we need it." Dana picked up her bags and carried them to a chair.

"Sounds like we'll have a hot meal and bath tonight. All the luxuries."

Dana smiled broadly. "Yes indeed. But before we do anything more we need to get our boots and socks off and let our feet breathe. Then pull out our supplies and clothing. Get them to drying."

She immediately went to work removing items from her backpack and supply pack. Travis followed her lead. Soon they had clothing spread out all over the place.

"The majority of my stuff is dry with the exception of my pants, socks and shoes." Travis slung his sleeping bag out across the bed.

She frowned. "And most of mine are wet."

He smiled. "That's what happens when you go swimming with them."

"Not funny. The night is warm. I'm going to hang a few of these things outside, like my sleeping bag and hope they dry some. The smaller stuff I'll put near the stove while I get together supper."

"I'll help you." He grabbed up a pile. "I saw a couple of folding chairs we could put to good use as a clothesline."

She held the door open for him as they went out into the twilight.

Travis nodded his head to the right. "The chairs are around that corner."

Dana led the way and set up the chairs. She then placed her belongings over them.

The pile was almost gone when Travis picked up a scrap of material. He held it at eye level. "Very sexy panties for fighting fires."

Dana snatched them out of his hand. "You're supposed to be helping not admiring my underwear."

He said as innocently as possible, "Hey, they just happened to pop out of the pile."

She huffed. "Okay, funny man, help me with this sleeping bag."

"What're we going to do with it?"

"I want to spread it over the rail." She picked up one end. He took the other. Together they laid it over the outside rail.

"I hope a good blow doesn't come up. They're going to find your belongings in Bend. I'd hate for another man to get to appreciate those panties."

She lightly slapped him on the arm as she went by him. "Have you thought of giving up medicine to do stand-up comedy?"

"I have not, but I just might now that you've encouraged me." He grinned.

"I am not encouraging you." She leaned toward him and glared up at him but a smile formed on her lips.

"That's what it sounded like to me."

Dana returned to straightening her sleeping bag. "Need to get your hearing checked too."

His voice dipped. "Oh, I hear just fine."

She headed toward the door, saying over her shoulder as she went, "Then hear this—I'm fixing dinner and if you want to eat something hot you better be nice to the cook."

He chuckled. "And here I was thinking I had been when I was admiring her panties."

She walked away muttering, "And we've circled back to that."

Dana liked that she and Travis had slipped back into what they'd had so long ago. He used to tease her unmercifully like she was his kid sister. Had that been how he saw her? Maybe she'd imagined there was more between them. He must've been shocked when she tried to kiss him. She'd been humiliated but he had to have been embarrassed, as well. She had never thought of it that way. Being unwanted one more time had been the only thing she could see. She'd been so naive.

It was nice to have her friend back. She hoped they remained that way. Travis kept her on her toes. His wit encouraged her to think, and even his questioning of her decisions made her listen to his views. She worked so hard in the smokejumping program to prove herself, she didn't dare show weakness. Maybe as he said, it wasn't always a sign of weakness to accept help.

Before getting started on their meal she pulled off her wet long-sleeve shirt leaving on her T-shirt. She laid her outer clothing across one of the chairs and turned on the propane heater. Everything she had was at best damp. She dreaded putting on clammy clothes after her shower, but it was that or walk around naked. The idea of her and Travis acting like Adam and Eve both shocked and intrigued her.

A few minutes later Travis looked over her shoulder. "It smells interesting."

She jumped at him being so near after such an erotic thought. If Travis had any idea what she'd been thinking... Gathering her thoughts she continued to stir the pot. "Is that a compliment?"

"It is. What can I do to help?"

"Grab one of the bags of fruit." She pointed to their supplies.

"I do love good dried fruit." He reached for a packet.

Dana grinned. "Why do I hear no sincerity in those words?"

"Maybe because there wasn't any."

She looked at him. "We'll be home soon. I promise."

"Hey, that wasn't really a complaint. I'll admit I like finer living then we've had for the last few days but I've liked getting to know you again."

"And I've liked getting to know you too." She turned back to the pot. "After dinner I need to check your arm, especially since it got wet."

"And you need another bandage. Yours went down the river." He touched her cheek.

A tingle ran through her. She chuckled and wobbled. "We're a needy pair."

"I know I am."

An odd note had entered Travis's voice making her look at him. He watched her, his eyes dark and wanting.

Dana shivered, yet her blood ran hot. She wasn't so inexperienced that she didn't recognize when a man desired her. That morning, half asleep and toasty warm, she'd wanted him too but now…here…

"I think I'll get a quick shower before dinner." With that he went out the door.

"But dinner's ready," she murmured to the empty air.

Fifteen minutes later at the sound of the door opening and closing she said, "Sit down. This is ready." She spooned the food onto the plates. Heading to the table, she jerked to a stop. Reality had come too close to her fancy. Travis sat at the table with no shirt on. She had a full view of a broad chest with a dusting of hair in the middle. His muscles flexed and relaxed as he picked up his water bottle, taking a swallow. The ripple of his throat fascinated her. She'd seen beautiful sunsets he outdid.

"Sorry about the no shirt and boxers at the table. My mother would have a fit but I couldn't bring myself to put those damp clothes on again."

Dana didn't move.

"Dana?"

Blinking to adjust the train of her thoughts, she placed the food on the table. Despite her hunger she didn't immediately eat. How was she expected to with a half-dressed Travis feet from her? He obviously wasn't having the same problem. He forked the food in as if it was the finest of meals.

"I'd like to enjoy the last of the sunset but I'm too hungry to take the time." He glanced up. "I don't know about you but this wouldn't be my normal fare but it sure does taste good. Nice and hot. Thank you."

"My pleasure." And she meant that. She didn't usually cook for a man, but somehow she liked doing the domestic things for Travis. "What would you be eating if you weren't here having this delicious meal?"

"I really like roast beef, mashed potatoes and gravy, creamed corn and lima beans and homemade rolls."

"Goodness. That's some list." She glanced at her plate. "This doesn't come close to that. Do you cook for yourself?"

"Not very much. I'm pretty good at breakfast. Eggs and bacon. I can make a mean macaroni and cheese out of the box."

She laughed. "I don't think that counts in the culinary world as cooking."

"Mostly I eat at the hospital or out. That was one of my and my ex's biggest disagreements. I wanted us to eat together. She liked to cook but there was never a meal when I got home. Don't get me wrong—I didn't think she should be a slave in the kitchen every night but it would've been nice to have a home-cooked meal waiting a few nights a week."

"I'd think you'd have women falling all over you to cook for you."

He turned his head to the side, lowered his chin and narrowed his eyes. "Actually, I don't. I don't want just anyone to do so. It was my mother's way of showing love. I guess I see it as a declaration of love."

"Oh." Dana looked at the plate again. She couldn't do that. What if he decided he didn't want her after all? She'd never recover from the pain, and she knew that type of pain too well.

Travis finished eating and sat back with a satisfied sigh. "I'll see to cleaning up while you get a shower."

"Thanks." Just before she left, Travis stopped her. "Hey, I have a dry T-shirt if you want it."

"That would be nice."

He went to his bag and pulled out a plastic bag, then removed a shirt.

She shook her head in disbelief as she took the clothing.

Travis made a proud lift to his chin. "A T-shirt can be used for a lot of things. To start a fire, as a towel, to filter water, carry berries, even be torn to make a rope."

"You continue to surprise me."

He watched her with hooded eyes. "I think I like that idea."

Not daring to continue that conversation, she headed outside. She couldn't get to the shower fast enough. Travis's brand of charm had her thinking about things better left alone.

Quickly showering, she realized she had nothing to dry off with so she stood there for a few moments to ring her hair out as much as she could, then using the T-shirt she took off to dry with. The last thing she needed to do was show up looking like she'd just been in a wet T-shirt contest. Grateful it had turned dark and there was still some heat from the day, she looked out at the stars. The lone dim lantern inside didn't ruin the view.

Would it really be so bad for her and Travis to act on what simmered between them? It might. There was a real chance her heart could get involved. All those old feelings she had for Travis had already come rushing back. But did he feel the same?

That morning she would've taken him any way she could have him. But that had been in the heat of the moment, the heat of him. She had the day to think rationally. Still, to have him for even a short time could only be wonderful. Was she strong enough to accept that? To risk the pain for a few moments of pleasure.

She went inside. Thankfully Travis's T-shirt almost reached her knees, covering her well. She went to check her drying clothes, touching them and flipping some.

"Dana, come to bed. If they dry, they dry. If not, we'll deal."

She turned to find Travis already lying on the single sleeping bag with his back to her. She'd wanted to rebandage his arm but would wait until morning. Moving the lantern to the floor near the bed, she turned it off and joined Travis. She lay stiffly beside him.

"Relax, Dana. I'm exhausted. When I make love to you we're both going to be well rested. Now sleep."

Dana released the breath she didn't know she had been holding, and closed her eyes.

Travis rolled and pulled the warm body snuggled against him closer. Legs intertwined with his as if Dana wanted to crawl inside him. He had no issue with that. Now fully awake, he couldn't stop himself from appreciating her heat pressed against him. She positioned her thigh across his. He couldn't resist brushing his fingertips over the exposed skin.

She nuzzled her face into his neck, then made the sweetest sound of pleasure. Her hand circled his waist. Her fingers brushed the waistband of his boxers, then wandered away leaving his manhood hard with need.

He kissed the top of her head as his hand cupped her butt, pressing her closer. The tip of her tongue touched his neck. His manhood throbbed. "Dana? Are you awake?"

"Mmm."

"Do you know what you're doing?" It might kill him if the answer wasn't what he wanted to hear.

"Dreaming?" She flexed her hips into his rock-hard length.

"That and other things."

She kissed his chest. "Do you always talk this much in bed?"

"No, I like to do other things much better. But I want you to understand that I can't offer you anything more than right now." His hand found her chin, then his mouth her lips. He had been wanting this for far too long.

"That's all I'm asking for. To be wanted. Right now." Dana's arms moved around his neck and she held him close.

"Sweetheart, I can promise you're wanted." Her lips were as full and luscious as he remembered. His intent had been a tender kiss but when Dana pulled him tighter his desire grew as his mouth became more demanding. He ran his tongue across her plush bottom lip.

She opened, welcomed him with her tongue.
Such sweetness.

His hand returned to her butt, pressing her
against his hardness. Reluctantly he broke the
kiss. "I didn't bring any protection."

"I'm on the Pill." She cupped his cheeks and
her mouth joined his.

Travis let her go long enough to remove
his boxers before sliding over Dana and between her legs. His hand glided up her thigh.
He pulled back. "No panties."

"Wet."

"If I had known…"

"Now you do." Her lips brushed his.

"Yes, I do." His mouth found hers again,
then floated over her cheek to nuzzle her ear.
"You want this?"

"Oh, yes." She flexed upward, her center
brushing the tip of his hard length.

With one thrust, Dana's heat surrounded
him, gripped him. Captured him. His mouth
ground into hers. She returned his passion. As
he plunged into her then pulled away, she rose
to meet him. Her fingers bit into his shoulders. When he feared he couldn't hold back any
longer Dana's body tensed, her hips rose. Her
mouth left his as that sweet sound he liked so
much rolled over her lips before she quivered
and sighed her joy.

He pounded into her, once, twice and thundered off into his own release. One so deeply satisfying he'd had no idea its kind existed. Having sex with Dana, he'd quickly found was far better than skydiving. Pulling her close, he closed his eyes and slept the sleep of a man well pleasured.

CHAPTER EIGHT

DANA WOKE TO just enough light so she could see. Travis's warmth surrounded her. She would never have thought two days ago she'd be lying next to Travis. Those feelings from years ago were still alive. Every man she'd dated she measured by Travis and they had come up wanting. She'd never dreamed he'd return to her life, but now that he had she'd take all of him he'd give her.

She hated to leave his arms but she needed to go downstairs to the outhouse. Sliding from under his arm, she climbed off the bed. Finding the T-shirt and her boots, she carried them outside to put them on. When she returned, Travis stood next to the outside rail with two mugs sitting beside him.

"Good morning. I found some coffee and thought it worth the use of our drinking water."

Dana hesitated. He acted as if it was a normal day. For her the world had shifted.

His gaze met hers—a smile covered his lips. He reached out an arm. "I missed you when I woke."

She stepped to him. His arm came around her waist, pulling her against him as his lips pressed against her temple. He handed her a mug then picked up the other before taking a sip. "I've heard of being just above the clouds but have never experienced it. I've had a number of firsts with you."

Dana looked out at the clouds so thick they appeared as if they could be walked on. The ground wasn't visible. The tops of the trees of a far-off mountain were all that could be seen. It was as if no one else existed in the world. "I've only seen it a couple of times but nothing as thick as this."

They stood sipping their coffee as the sun slowly burnt off the mist.

Travis set his mug down, took hers and did the same. He came to stand behind her. His hands wrapped her waist as he pulled her back against him. The hard length of him pressing into her behind. She moved to turn. His mouth nuzzled her ear. "Hold the rail, Dana. I wish to give you the devotion you deserve but I self-ishly didn't take time to give you last night."

"But I want—"

"Shh. Just feel."

His hands went to the hem of the T-shirt. Pulling it up, they traveled along her sides until they cupped her breasts. He lifted, and gently squeezed them. "So perfect." His lips muttered against her ear before they teased the hollow behind her ear.

She leaned her head to the side so he had better advantage. Heat pooled heavy at her center.

His fingers traced her nipples, teased them then tugged until they were hard nibs. His palms came to rest over them. She squirmed, her knees becoming weak.

His tongue traced the shell of her ear. Dana hummed low in her throat. She had turned as tight as a violin string and he strummed her.

She reached around him before grabbing his thighs. That only brought him nearer making her more aware of his rock-hard manhood. Still his skillful hands continued to do magical things to her breasts.

Her mouth fell open as her breaths turned to pants. She returned her hands to the rail so she wouldn't fall as pleasure rocked her.

Travis continued to leave tiny kisses along her hairline as one of his hands went to her middle, locking her against him while his fingers brushed her curls on the way to her center. Involuntarily she widened her legs, throbbing for his attention. He stopped just before slipping into her wet and waiting heat. He retreated.

Dana moaned her protest. Her center pulsed, begging for his touch. Her fingers turned white where they gripped the rail. She flexed against Travis, her body pleading for his continued devotion.

His lips moved to the curve of her neck as his hand returned to her center. All her concentration, her blood, focused on her center, the pounding need to have Travis's attention.

His fingertips caressed her swollen center. That wasn't enough. She arched chasing his touch.

"Turn around, sweetheart. I want to see you come against the sunrise."

Dana did as he asked but only with his help. She gripped his forearms.

"Lean back, sweetheart." One of his arms lay along the rail. "I've got you."

Dana did as he asked. She would have done anything he asked.

Travis pushed at the T-shirt, baring her breasts, and looked at her. "So beautiful." His mouth took one of her nipples and sucked as his finger entered her.

She bucked. It was as if a lightning strike had hit her sending its power zipping through her. She closed her eyes and felt. Travis's mouth continued to caress her breasts as his finger teased her nub. A tightness built, twisted, curled then pleaded for release. Dana threw back her head, pressed against the rail and down on Travis's masterful hand before screaming her release. She shuddered as it echoed in the morning air.

When her knees failed to hold her, Travis brought her against him. He held her tenderly. After a few minutes she stepped back still steadying herself with hands on his biceps.

He looked into her eyes. "Thank you for that gift. It was the most amazing experience of my life."

Dana's cheeks heated and she looked away.

Using a curled finger, Travis raised her chin so she had to meet his gaze. "You're an extraordinary woman, Dana Warren." He kissed her softly.

She wrapped her arms around his waist and pulled him tight, kissing him deeply. "I need you in me."

With a swift turn, he had her pinned against the glass. Seconds later his boxers were on the catwalk. Minutes later the birds flew from the trees at the roar of her name across Travis's lips.

* * *

Travis watched from the bed for a peep of Dana's naked sweet butt beneath his T-shirt as she checked the clothing to see if it was dry. Could a morning get any better than this? "You know, I really did think about you through the years."

Her gaze shot to meet his. "You did?"

"You're not that easy to forget." That brought a small smile to her face.

"I thought about you, as well. What did you wonder about me?"

He leaned up on an elbow to see her better. "At first I wondered how bad I had hurt your feelings. Then I just wondered where you were. If you were happy." His voice took on a soft note. "You should know it's never wrong to let someone know you care about them. I really am sorry I hurt you."

"You didn't mistreat me. I had a crush." She kept messing with the clothes. "As I've already said, it was the heat of the moment."

"I was a self-centered young man who thought he had his whole world planned out. Was doing what he'd been told would get him ahead in the world." That was exactly what he had been doing. He'd not realized that until now. Not once had he thought about what he really wanted. Why did he feel he had to follow some established plan for his life? Why hadn't he thought about what made him happy?

"That's all a long time ago." She continued moving clothes around. "We need to get started."

"I don't see why we can't spend the day here. Head out tomorrow." Travis patted the bed and grinned.

She returned it. "As much as I'd like that idea, I don't think the forest service wants to pay me for spending all day in bed with you."

"Is there any reason we can't leave in an hour?" He winked. Dana started toward him. Her focus left him to look out the window behind him and she jerked to a stop.

He rolled, looking out, as well. "What's wrong?"

"Smoke." Her voice had lost it humor.

"There was no electrical storm."

"Most likely a careless camper." She jerked on her panties, then pulled off the T-shirt put on the bra and returned the shirt. Finding her pants, she stepped into them.

Dana had morphed into firefighter mode. What he'd hoped for wasn't going to happen.

"No matter how many times we say no burning, no campfires this time of the year someone inevitably ends up letting one get out of hand." She picked up the radio and headed for the door. "I'm calling base."

Travis rolled out of bed and started dressing.

Dana returned. "So far they haven't seen the smoke so it's still small. Since I'm so close I need to go see about it. Maybe it's just a campfire. You can head on out. All you have to do is follow the road. It's a walk but it reaches a main road. I can radio in and have someone pick you up."

"Not going to happen. I'm going with you." Travis started packing his bags.

"You don't have to."

His gaze met hers. "You're not going alone."

Her look of surprise took him off guard. "Is something wrong?"

Her eyes were bright. "No, I'm just not used to someone being that concerned about me."

He took her hand and pulled her gently to him. "What're friends for?" He kissed her and patted her on the butt. "Now let's get moving. We've a fire to see about."

She grinned, turned and picked up her belongings.

"Can't we leave some of these supplies here? Travel lighter. Come back for them."

"No, they have to go with us. We may not be back this way."

* * *

Fifteen minutes later they had their packs on. "Let's go. If it's any consolation there's no water to cross on this trip."

"I do love dry feet." He hadn't let on to her what bad shape his feet were in. If he had she would've insisted he stay behind. He'd patched himself up with the supplies he had and put on two pairs of socks. Had also taken two pain relievers while she was outside seeing to the stuff hanging there. "I'm ready when you are."

They headed down the stairs. At the bottom, Dana checked with base for more information and confirmed GPS coordinates of the fire. She set a steady pace as they walked across the field into the woods.

"How far away do you think it is?"

"Couple of miles. It shouldn't take long to get there."

Thoughts of their earlier activities kept him from thinking about his feet. He wanted to repeat them. Bring that look of delight to Dana's face again.

Dana hated she hadn't gotten Travis back to town before going off to another fire. He was a doctor not a firefighter. She'd tried to leave him behind, but from the determined look in his eyes he wasn't going to let that happen. Her heart had swelled at his support but she'd seen the gingerly way he walked. His feet pained him.

She'd glanced in the window when she'd been out on the catwalk and seen him caring for his feet. Taking longer than necessary, she gave him time to finish before she announced they should go. She hated Travis was hurt but she didn't have time to argue with him about going or not.

They broke into an open area of small bushes with an occasional tree. Travis came up beside her. Smoke filled the air. "Let's hope it hasn't gotten out of hand by the time we get there."

"I'll second that." To go home for a rest and hot bath sounded good right now. She glanced at Travis. Yet she'd miss him when they got back. But that had been the plan.

This morning on the catwalk had been unbelievable. Too many orgasms like that and her heart might burst. That Travis had given it to her only made it sweeter. It would be a precious memory of their time together.

Once again she smelled the fire before she saw it. Moving forward they found the scorched black burn line. "It looks as if we've caught it early. We need to get out in front of it and make a fire line. Stop it before it crawls any farther.

I only have half a tank of gas left for the chain saw. We have to plan its use carefully."

"Hey!" A young man who looked in his early twenties came running toward them waving his hands above his head. "I'm glad to see you." He coughed. "Can you help us?"

"What's wrong?" Dana asked.

The man pointed behind him toward some rocks that had just been missed by the fire. "My friend broke his leg."

Travis turned to her. "I'll check on him then come help you. I want you to stay within my eyesight until I can get to you."

She nodded.

"If you don't promise to do as I say, I'm coming with you right now." Travis narrowed his eyes and watched her closely.

He'd make that kind of choice for her? No one outside her grandfather ever had and he hadn't wanted to. She'd been pretty much thrust into his lap.

"I'll do my best. But it's my job."

Travis's look bored into hers. Then he nodded. "Good enough."

As he and the guy hurried away she heard Travis say, "I'm a doctor. Tell me how your friend got hurt."

The wind picked up and the smoke grew

heavier as she approached the fire. She pulled her bandanna up over her mouth and started to work on a firebreak.

Once she'd glanced back to see Travis standing up and looking her direction as if searching the area. Apparently he saw her because he sat down again beside his patient. Half an hour later, he joined her as she worked the dirt with her Pulaski.

"The hurt guy?"

Travis joined in right beside her. "He's settled out of harm's way, leaning against a tree. I told both guys to stay put and we'd be back for them. I had the guy lay your damp sleeping bag and our clothes out in the sun."

"Really?"

"Yeah, we're going to need them to get the hurt one to help. I also figured we might have to spend another night out here."

"It's starting to look that way." She picked up the pace and he did the same.

It was the middle of the afternoon when they stopped and surveyed their progress. Travis stood with his gloved hands on the top of his Pulaski handle. She surveyed the black area around them, having already gone down on her hands and knees to test for any heat in the soil.

"It looks like we got it." Dana pulled her bandanna down and wiped her face on her sleeve.

"Yeah, it does."

She looked at Travis. He studied her. She asked, "What's wrong?"

"I was just thinking how completely inappropriate it would be to kiss you but I really want to."

She licked her lips and stepped to him. "It might be, but I'd sure like one."

Travis took her in his arms; his mouth touched hers with such gentleness she almost cried. She clung to him. His lips were a caress pressed against hers. When she would've taken the kiss deeper he kept it tender as if he was trying to express the depth of his feelings. Her arm went around his neck while another lay on his chest. His heart beat solid and sure beneath her hand.

Heaven help her, she would miss him when their time was over.

He pulled back, placing his black-from-smoke-and-dirt forehead against hers. After taking a deep breath, he let it out slowly. "As much as I wish we were going to be alone again tonight, I think we need to get back to my patient. We've got to work out some arrangement for getting him to a hospital."

"Can't we call in Rescue?" Dana picked up the chain saw sitting not far away.

"We could but it'll be dark before they could

make it this far today. If the weather doesn't turn maybe they could make it in the morning. I still think we need to plan to get him out of here on our own."

"Agreed. Do you think the guys will be where you left them?"

"Yeah." Travis took her hand and held it as they went as if they were strolling in a park. She couldn't help but smile at the picture they must make. Nasty, sweaty and dusty from head to toe. "They were both too scared to move. Especially when I told them you work for the forest service. They knew they were in trouble then."

"Ah, I get to be the bad guy."

He grinned. "Someone's gotta do it."

As they walked up to the guys, the mobile one came running to them. "I was afraid you had forgotten about us."

She tried to pull her hand from Travis's but he hung on to it.

"No. It just takes time to put out a fire," Travis said not slowing down until they reached the injured fellow. "Ted," Travis indicated the man with a broken leg, "and Jim, this is Dana Warren, a smokejumper with the US Forest Service."

"Ah, hi." Jim shrugged. "Sorry about the fire."

Ted gave her a weak smile. His eyes were glazed over in pain.

Travis choked back a chuckle as she glared at Jim.

"We just had a small campfire. We had to cook." The guy's voice climbed higher with each word. "I don't know how it got out. It became a brush fire like that." He snapped his fingers. "We tried to stop it but we couldn't. Everything we did made it worse. I got burnt then Jim fell and broke his leg."

After her initial disgust, Dana couldn't help but feel sorry for the guy despite him not following the law during fire season. She pursed her lips and shook her head. Young and stupid. She looked at Travis. She'd been that once. Was she now being older and stupid?

He looked at her and raised a brow. Was he thinking the same thing?

"Do you have any water?" Travis asked.

Jim said, "Yeah. Right here. We managed to save a few of our supplies. Our parents would kill us if we'd lost their stuff."

Dana rolled her eyes. Apparently they'd been more concerned with saving their butts instead of the forest. Jim went around the tree and returned with an armload of camping equipment including two CamelBak canteens.

Travis leaned his Pulaski against the tree

and went down on his knees beside Ted and said in a calm, reassuring voice, "We're going to need to get this splinted and secured so we can get you out of here. You'll be fine."

Dana's heart filled with pride. After fighting a fire for the last six hours, kissing her like she was the most precious person in the world, Travis was now caring for his patient. He was the most amazing man. She hadn't been wrong all those years ago. He had been special then and he still was.

Travis sighed as he looked at Ted's leg. What he wouldn't give if he and Dana were on their way back to the fire tower. Even their gentle kiss had left him wanting more. He spoke to Ted. "I'm going to need to cut your pants so I can see more clearly what's going on."

"Okay." Ted's eyes were glassy with pain. The over-the-counter pain reliever wasn't doing much for him.

Travis looked at Jim. "You go find two solid limbs that I can use for splints. Make them as long as your leg."

"Dana, would you check on a helicopter then come help me?"

"Ten-four." A few minutes later she returned to stand beside him.

"So can they send one?" Travis asked over his shoulder.

"You were right. Not this late in the day. Tomorrow morning at the earliest. But they are expecting another front with high winds. They'll let us know if they can make a pickup."

Disappointment filled Travis as he looked back at his patient. "Just as I thought. Then we'll have to work as if we are going to have to carry him out of here. We need to clean up some if I'm going to work with his leg." He picked up his pack and carried it far enough away they had some privacy.

Dana followed him.

He pulled out his now well-used T-shirt and wet it before handing it to her.

She wiped her face and cleaned her hands. "Kind of makes you wish for a good river doesn't it?"

He grinned. "That it does. What I'm dreaming of is a hot shower with you." Dana rewarded him with pink coming to her cheeks even through the dirt. "You make me want to kiss you when you blush."

She handed him the T-shirt. "Clean your face, Dr. Russell, and I'll pour water over your hands." She took the bottle from him.

With Dana's help he managed to get his

hands fresh enough he felt he could care for a patient.

"What do you want me to do?"

"Go through our supplies and theirs and find anything that can be cut up to be used as wrapping on the leg. I want you to help me with that when Jim returns. Do you think we can make it back to the tower before it turns dark?"

Dana looked at the sun. "I'd hate to chance it if we're carrying an injured person."

"That what I was thinking. We make camp here tonight and build something to carry Ted out with just in case we need it."

"I can get Jim started on that when he gets back. I'll cut some limbs and we'll make a travois, like the Native Americans used to move their goods with. Will that work?"

Travis smiled, and nodded. "That would be brilliant."

"We'll cut the ropes off the parachutes to strap the poles together and use them to create the bed for him to lie on. The sleeping bag on top should make it as comfortable as possible."

"Sounds like a plan. If Rescue can't get here we'll walk him out and have someone at the tower to meet us."

"Agreed."

Jim came running toward them. "I've got them." He held up a stick in each hand.

"Put them over there near Ted. We've another job for you." Travis went to his supply bag and pulled out his parachute. "Cut the ropes off of this. Make them as long as possible." He handed the material to Jim.

"Did you guys parachute in here?" His eyes went wide with disbelief.

"Yes, we did," Dana said evenly.

Travis took a deep breath. "Do you have a knife?"

"Yep." Jim showed him.

"Then get to work." Travis pointed toward the bags.

"Dana, will you come help me, please." Travis went down on his knees beside Ted. "I'm going to need you at his feet."

Dana went to the ground also.

"Ted, I'm going to remove these temporary splints. Then I'm going to have to cut your pants."

"Pretty ingenious splinting there, Doc," Dana said.

Travis gave her a thin-lipped grin. He'd used part of a thin flexible tent pole from the guys' tent. "Thanks. It's what I had in a pinch but he needs something sturdier if we plan to move him. That's why I sent Jim out for limbs."

From behind Travis Jim said, "Yeah, but my

dad's going to be mad when he finds out it's broken."

"And your dad isn't going to be happy to learn you started a forest fire either." Travis was on the road to losing patience with the dense kid.

Carefully, Travis removed the splinting, then took scissors from his medical pack and cut up the inside seam of Ted's pants. When he could pull the material back enough, he examined the injured area. The break was just below the knee.

"It looks as if both the tibia and the fibula are broken. Without X-rays I couldn't be certain. We'll just have to treat it as the worst-case scenario." The area around it had turned a vivid red and blue. "The bone hasn't come through the skin. We need to see that it doesn't."

It would be tricky to do so with the rough ride Ted would have the next morning but Travis could only do his best.

"Dana, while I'm getting everything we need together would you mind taking his vitals. The last thing we need is Ted starting to run a fever."

"Jim, stop what you're doing and find another tent pole. I need it as well for splinting." Travis called over his shoulder.

Dana picked up his medical bag and went to Ted's head.

Jim grumbled but did as he was told. Travis took the pole, then cut the elastic cord that held them together, giving him two poles to work with.

"Temp is normal. Heartrate is elevated and pulse is, as well," Dana reported.

"Not a surprise since he's in pain. Come down to his feet now. I want you to put your elbows on the ground and support his calf between your forearms while I put more splints on. First, I'm going to wrap the area then reapply the splints."

Picking up one of the guys' shirts, Travis ripped a sleeve off. He wrapped it around the injured area. "I want this to support and not restrict blood flow." He spoke more to himself than to the others. He picked up another sleeve and applied it. "Now for the tent poles."

Dana straightened and rolled her shoulders before assuming her position again.

Travis placed one between Ted's legs. "I'm going to tie these off then I want to put one on the back and front of his leg." He looked at Dana. "I'll need you to help me with tying those." He picked up a strip of cloth.

"Okay, Dana. Now I need you to pull the end of the cloth through when I push it under his thigh." He did so and she pulled it up. Putting the last two poles in place, he tied them down. "Now let's do the lower part of the leg."

By the time he and Dana were through manipulating the leg Ted's lips were white and his eyes closed. That was a good thing. Travis had very little to give him as pain reliever. He had one dose of hydrocodone left that he'd brought for Mr. Gunter. He wanted to save it to give Ted in the morning. His ride out would be painful.

Travis patted Ted's shoulder. "I'm sorry I can't do anything more."

"I appreciate what you have done." Ted mumbled.

Dana brushed the hair back from the guy's face. She looked at Travis and her eyes were dark with concern. Dana had a tender heart. She picked up her supply bag and put it under Ted's good leg.

"Good thinking," Travis said. "It'll help prevent shock."

Dana picked up a nearby sleeping bag and opened it before placing it over Ted.

"Let's get the travois made before it gets dark."

"Jim," Travis called. "We're going to need your help."

The guy looked up from where he removed

the lines from the parachute canopy. A pile of rope lay beside him.

"I need you to go with Dana. She'll show you what to do."

Without a word Dana picked up the chain saw and started into the woods.

The thing he liked best about Dana was that he could trust her. She didn't think about herself first. His ex-wife had always questioned how it would affect her. Dana was resilient. The last few days had been tough and she weathered them well. With her, he knew what it was like to have a true partner. Not just in name only.

Despite their earlier disagreements they had become friends. Real ones. The kind who could trust each other through thick and thin. The golden ones that were hard to come by. Lovers could come and go but someone who you could trust was rare, to be valued.

Dana was no shrinking violet nor was she somebody who had to have everyone's attention. She shone despite her efforts not to. Her confidence came from her skills and her love of life. She earned that the hard way. Life hadn't always been kind to her but she'd kept on moving forward, following her dream. Could he say the same about himself?

He rechecked Ted's vitals. The grind of the

saw came from not far off. He went to work to see about their supplies and repacking the ones that were dry. Thankfully most of them were. He was glad to see Jim had left Dana's panties in her bag. Those he should be the only male allowed to touch.

Soon Dana and Jim returned. He pulled two limbs along behind him. Dana did the same with one about half the length of the others.

Dana seat the chain saw down and spoke to Jim. "Lay yours parallel to each other. Then cross one end over the other." Jim did as she said. She then laid the pole she'd carried over the poles a foot from the ends of the others. The poles made a triangle. When they were done one person would be able to pull or the three of them could carry when necessary.

Travis picked up the rope Jim had cut and joined them.

"We need to get these tied off." Dana took a rope from him and started tying the crossed poles by weaving in and out and around.

Travis took one and started working it around one of the bottom intersections.

Dana said to the watching Jim, "Look through that pile and find the longest pieces."

Jim went to work.

Travis finished off the intersection he'd been working on and started on the other.

When he finished Dana said, "Jim, bring a rope and come help me." He did. "I'm going to tie it off over here, then pass it to you and I want you to wrap it around twice and pass it back to me. We're going to zigzag it all the way to the end. We'll tie the rope together as we go until we have created a bed."

Jim grinned. "This is so rad."

Travis stopped himself from rolling his eyes. Had he been this unaware when he'd been Jim's age? He looked at Dana. He feared he might have been.

"With the give of the rope we'll make Ted as comfortable as we can." Dana gave her work on the travois the same focus she did everything. Done, she went to the front, turned around, putting her hand behind her and holding the poles she pulled. It worked great.

Travis decided then she wouldn't be doing the pulling when the time came.

Dana looked at him. "What do you think?"

"I think you do good work." Once again she'd impressed him.

She smiled broadly. His heart swelled. He made a mental reminder to brag on her often.

"What're we gonna do with it?" Jim asked.

He and Dana looked at each other, then back at Jim.

Travis said with as even a tone as he could

manage, "We're gonna put Ted on it and you and I are going to take turns pulling him out of here if we have to."

"Oh."

"Dana, please pull it over beside Ted. I'd like to get him off the ground for the night if we can. Jim, come help us."

Dana put the travois down and picked up one of the guys' sleeping bags. Opening it, she laid it over the ropes leaving enough to cover Ted with.

"Jim," Travis squatted down beside Ted, "get across Ted from me. We're going to lift Ted while he's still unconscious. He'd be in real pain if we did it while he was awake. The longer he's out the better for him."

"What do I need to do?" Dana asked.

"I want you to hold his broken leg as level as possible."

"Now, Jim, slide a hand under his shoulders. I'll slide mine under his lower back and we lift on three."

Everyone moved to their positions.

"Ready? On three. One, two, three," Travis called.

Between the three of them they managed to get Ted where Travis wanted him. Ted did moan but settled quickly. He just did fit in the space they had made for him.

"You guys lift this end and let me get this pack under his feet again." Dana situated the pack on the ground beneath one end of the travois.

"Good job." Dana pulled the sleeping bag over Ted and tucked it in.

"I'm hungry," Jim announced. "What're we going to eat for supper without a campfire?"

Travis walked over to his pack and pulled out a bag of MREs. He tossed it to Jim. "Bon appétit."

"What?" Jim gave him an odd look.

Travis had had enough. He and Dana had been at it since sunup and he was hungry and tired. "Just open it and eat." He pulled out two more bags. He looked at Dana. "What would you like? Vegetables and roast beef or vegetables and roast beef."

She gave him a tired smile. "I guess vegetables and roast beef it is."

Travis handed her two packages. Dana sat down where she was. Travis got their water and joined her.

"This is dried-up food." Jim sounded as if he was being asked to eat worms.

"Yeah, but wasn't it you who tried to start a cook fire in a 'no fire' time of year?" Travis couldn't stop himself from saying.

Jim had the good grace to look ashamed.

Dana ate without saying much. She looked exhausted and had a right to be. The bandage on her face had long ago fallen off. He'd kept her up during the night and they'd risen early that morning. They'd walked a distance through the woods to then put out a fire before caring for an injured person. She'd earned her rest.

Jim stood nearby looking awkward.

Dana patted the ground next to her. "Jim, come sit with us and tell us where you live."

The guy wiggled like a puppy as he joined them. Dana had that effect on people. If gruff old Mr. Gunter had warmed to her then anyone could. What made her special was she didn't work at it or realize it. She was genuine in her caring.

Soon the sun had gone behind the mountains.

Dana stood. "I'm going to get some sleep. I've had a long day. Tomorrow we'll either meet the helicopter or walk out of here. Either way we'll have to be up at daylight."

She stuffed her water bottle and paper wrapper in her bag.

"Daylight?" Jim echoed.

Travis pursed his lips. That was it for him. "You do realize that you started a forest fire today that burnt land that belongs to all of us.

Your friend is seriously injured. He needs to be in a hospital and will need an operation. He has a painful trip ahead of him."

Dana stepped up beside Travis and placed her hand on his arm. "It's time we all got some rest."

Travis looked at her. She gave him a slight smile. Without another word he went to where he'd left their sleeping bags rolled on top of the parachute canopy. He opened one bag and laid it out. He then unzipped hers, placing it on top of his. Dana didn't ask any questions about the arrangement. She took off her boots and outside shirt, climbed under the top bag and removed her pants. He did the same. As far as he was concerned Jim could fend for himself.

Travis pulled Dana to him. She resisted for a moment but he slipped his arm under her head and kissed her temple. She soon rolled to her side, and snuggled against his chest.

"Hell of a day to start it out so sweetly," he whispered.

"Uh-huh."

"Good night, sweetheart." His arm rested around her waist. Despite the way the day had gone, he liked the ending. Having Dana in his arms seemed right. He closed his eyes to the sound of her soft easy breathing.

CHAPTER NINE

DANA CLUNG TO the warmth. Not wanting to wake.

"Dana, it's almost sunrise."

She even liked that voice.

She burrowed closer to the warmth.

"Sweetheart, you keep that up and we're going to put on a show for these guys."

Her eyes opened wide.

Travis grinned. He stood and pulled his pants on but not before she saw his manhood standing tall and proud behind his boxers. She groaned. Grabbing her pants, she pulled them on while inside the sleeping bag and stood.

Travis took her in his arms.

"We can't," she said looking around him.

He frowned. "Can't I at least get a good morning kiss?"

She smiled and put her arms around his neck. "That I'll do."

Travis's mouth met hers as if he was a dying

man and she could save him. One of his hands went to her butt and pulled her tight against him. "Feel what you do to me?"

His kiss promised more when they were alone. But that wouldn't happen. They were going home today. And their own ways. He'd not said anything about seeing her again. She hadn't either. They both were adults and knew the score. With that thought she tightened her hold and kissed him deeply. With a groan, he released her, but acting as reluctant to let her go as she was to have him do so. So quickly she'd become attuned to him.

Sometime during the night he'd gotten out of bed. She'd woken missing his warmth and hard body holding hers. There had been enough moonshine she could see him checking on Ted.

"Is everything okay?" she'd asked.

Travis returned to bed pulling her close. "Shh. Everything's fine. Go back to sleep."

Just like that she had. As if Travis telling her things were fine made it so. He'd take care of her and everyone else, as well. She loved the security he provided when she'd had so little in her life.

As soon as he'd dressed, Travis left her and went to Ted, and started taking his vitals. The kid's lips were tight with pain. While Travis saw to Ted she stepped away to talk to base about the helicopter. She soon returned.

Travis looked at her. "What're the arrangements? When will the helicopter be here?"

She pursed her lips and shook her head. "No time soon. Best they can do it midmorning. There're only two copters and both are out on runs for more urgent cases. We'd come out better time wise by carrying him out."

Travis closed his eyes. "And every day brings another adventure."

Dana hurried to break camp. She noticed Travis using a syringe to give Ted an injection in his arm.

"What's that you're giving him?"

"Hydrocodone. I'd brought this with me in case I needed it for Mr. Gunter."

"I'm glad you had some left. I'm afraid Ted will need it." She smiled down at the guy.

He was so miserable he didn't even try to return it.

"My thought too." Travis took the guy's arm, prepared it for a shot and expertly inserted the needle. Afterward Travis offered Ted something to drink. "We don't need you dehydrated."

Jim grumbled when he had to get up. Only when Travis threatened to leave him did Jim start moving. "Maybe Ted and I should've gone to the beach."

Travis nodded. "Yeah, I think you guys should give that some thought next time you're planning a trip. Get your stuff together and let's get moving. Don't leave anything behind."

Travis joined her at the front of the travois. He leaned in close. "Let's get this guy," he nodded toward Jim, "out of here before he dies despite our best efforts to save him."

Dana rolled her eyes. "I know what you mean. If he wasn't so innocent I'd see that the book was thrown at them."

"I'll take first turn pulling," Travis announced. "Jim, you carry the supplies." Travis picked up the poles and they headed out.

They'd not traveled far when Dana was glad Travis had given Ted pain medicine. Bumping over the ground as he was, he could only be in agony.

They started their return trip to the fire tower because that was where someone would be waiting on them. The tower had the nearest road. It was slow and arduous journey. While they crossed open spaces, Travis pulled. When they came to the trees and the upward grade Travis had Jim take the front while she and

Travis carried the back. He also made sure to handle the chain saw, as well.

The trip would've been easier if it hadn't been for the moaning and groaning of Jim but he did keep moving. Dana wasn't sure if it was from his fear of Travis or from the fact that he knew if he kept going there would eventually be an end to the misery. Ted thankfully slept.

Travis called a halt for rest a number of times, not only for themselves but for Ted. What should've been a two-hour trip turned into a four-hour one. It was with great relief she saw the fire tower across the open field. With the tower in sight, Jim managed to find new energy and pick up the pace.

She was even happier to see the light green forest service truck base had told her to expect. Dana casually knew the female ranger waiting. She'd brought fresh water which was eagerly accepted. The road into the fire tower had been determined too rough for an ambulance. They'd meet it at the ranger station out on the main road. It took some time to settle Ted in the bed of the pickup truck to Travis's satisfaction. He climbed in the back beside the young man.

"Jim, ride back here. I'll need your help to steady Ted."

Dana took the open seat in the cab. She spent much of the ride looking through the window to check on the passengers in the back. More times than not Travis and Jim were holding the travois poles up so the going would be easier for Ted.

Once she caught Travis's attention and he winked at her. Her stomach fluttered. He had a way of making her feel all woman. Like a girl crazy about a guy. One she soon wouldn't be seeing any more. They'd agreed to short-term.

Over the bumpy, often washed-out road it took them almost an hour to reach the paved street and another thirty minutes to arrive at the rangers' station. There the ambulance waited.

As they pulled in, the EMTs were ready with the stretcher. Jim's and Ted's parents were there, as well. She and Travis quickly became busy, making it difficult for them to talk. She focused on the parents while Travis gave a report to the EMTs as he oversaw Ted being moved to the stretcher.

With what she needed to say to the parents finished, Dana moved away letting them fuss over their sons. She stood beside the ranger truck and watched the EMTs load Ted into the ambulance.

Travis walked over to her. "I've got to go with Ted."

"I figured you would. I've got to go to my office."

"Dr. Russell, are you coming?" One of the EMTs called as he held one of the back doors open.

"Be right there." Travis gave her one last look of regret and a wave as he loped off and climbed into the ambulance.

A heaviness fell over her as if she was being smothered. Tears formed but she checked them before they rolled. What they'd found together had just slipped out of her hands. Travis was gone again. They were in the real world once more. Things were different there.

But that was how it was supposed to happen. He didn't want forever. She had her safe life where she wouldn't get hurt. So why did it matter so much? It was time to get back to the life she'd built.

Dana looked at the ranger. "I'm ready to go."

"Sounds like you and the doctor had a few wild days together," the ranger said as she pulled out into the road.

"Yeah. It was interesting at times." Days that she'd like to have back.

"Also sounds like you and Dr. Russell made a pretty good team."

"We did." Especially in bed. She already missed him. But that was then and this was now. He'd said nothing about calling her. She hadn't asked. Hadn't had a chance. Or was it fear over what he might answer? She refused to have a repeat of what had happened years before. This time she would handle her feelings better.

At the station she pulled out her supply bag and Travis's, as well. After returning their equipment to Cache, she went to the locker room and took a long hot shower. As nice as it was, her thoughts were about the cold ones she'd had while with Travis. The smoke still clung to her hair as she blew it dry. As long as it stayed it would remind her of her time with Travis.

In the main office she found an open computer and wrote up her report being as detailed as possible but leaving out how close she and Travis had become. Reliving it through words only made the loss sharper.

On her way out, she stuck her head into Leo's office.

He looked up. "Hey, good to see you."

"It's nice to be back. You should have my report in your email."

His brows rose. "I understand you've had an interesting few days."

She shrugged and held the door frame tighter. "That'd be an understatement."

"Your trail crew is already in."

"That's what I heard." She had forgotten about them as her days with Travis had lengthened.

"I'm giving you and them a few days to rest up before I put you back in the rotation."

"Okay."

Leo's eyes narrowed. "No argument?"

She shook her head. "Nope."

He studied her a moment. "Is there something I need to know?"

She pursed her lips. "No."

Leo still studied her. "If that changes let me know. See you on Thursday ready to go up again."

"I'll be here." She made her way out to her truck.

Just a few days before, her ranch had been her haven. The place she went to reenergize. Now she dreaded being alone. There would be too much time to relive the hours with Travis, his kisses, those explosive moments on the catwalk, the look in his eyes when he desired her...

She'd known better than to get involved with him. He'd never once promised her anything. What had happened between them had all been the heat of the moment. Convenience. But for her…he'd gotten under her skin, again. She liked the guy outside of bed and in. They had rekindled their friendship. For that she was grateful.

Travis hadn't liked leaving Dana like he did. He would much rather have gone back to the station with her, hustled her through whatever paperwork she had to do and then followed her home into a shared hot shower, and then bed, with some sexual fun in both places. He sighed. Sadly that hadn't been how things worked out or been their agreement.

A night of passion had been the deal. He would honor that. But it would be difficult. He wanted more of Dana.

With his report about his care of Ted to the ER doctor finished, Travis waited with Ted and his parents until he had been wheeled into the OR to have his leg set. Eager to get away so he could clean up and possibly see Dana, he got a ride to the smokejumper station. To his disappointment, Dana had already gone for the night and the office was closed except for the dispatcher. He asked the woman for Dana's number but she told him she wasn't allowed to give that information out.

Maybe it was just as well. Travis rubbed his hand across his jaw. He needed a shave. To get some good sleep. Dana needed the rest, as well. His feared when he had a soft mattress with a good hot meal in his belly he might not be able to sleep well without Dana beside him.

He had learned one thing on their big adventure. That since his divorce he'd closed himself off to life. He'd been so fearful of making plans and being disappointed that he'd quit thinking about the future. His personal life had become an endless stream of no emotional attachments. If he didn't care then he didn't get hurt. But was that a healthy way to live?

A half an hour later while standing under the water he wondered how Dana was doing. In bed, he tossed and turned. How swiftly he'd become used to having her next to him. Maybe she'd be willing to extend their agreement. She might even call him. If not, he'd give her a few days and call her. Ask her how she was doing. If she'd recovered from their trip. With his first plan that had something to do with a woman in a long time in mind, he went to bed with a smile on his face.

The next morning he called to check on Mr. Gunter's progress and to see how Ted was doing. He received good reports. Then there was a week's worth of work to tackle and patients to see.

Two days went by and he still hadn't heard from Dana. He called the station, determined to check on her. The person who answered told him she was there but couldn't come to the phone right then. He left a message for her to call him.

When he hadn't heard from her by late afternoon he phoned the station again. "This is Dr. Russell. May I speak to Dana?"

"I think she's around here somewhere. Hold on a minute."

He paced across his small office. Since when had he been so nervous about calling a woman? Dana was already messing with his ordered life. He made another three trips across the floor before she came to the phone.

"Hi, Dana. It's Travis."

"Hey." An unsure note surrounded the word.

"I was just calling to check on you. See if you've recovered from our adventures."

"I'm fine. How about you?"

The warmth in her voice had returned. Suddenly this call had taken on more importance. "I'm great. Still sore but getting better every day." He cleared his throat. "I'd like to see you."

There was a pause. "This is fire season. I never know my schedule."

His heart sank. "I understand. Maybe another time."

"If you wouldn't mind coming to my place…"

"I'll bring supper and we can eat it on your porch." He wasn't going to give her time to change her mind.

"Does six work?"

"That's fine." Why did she sound so unsure? Their last morning together she had been warm and responsive to his kiss. He'd like to hear more enthusiasm in her voice. Was she afraid of him? He didn't like that idea.

She gave him her address.

"I'm looking forward to seeing you." His voice softened as he gripped the phone.

"Me too."

That note of anticipation he'd been looking for turned up in those two words. He said goodbye with a smile on his face. It shouldn't matter so much to him. He had been the one who had said he wouldn't be offering more.

As he drove along Dana's gravel lane three hours later, Travis couldn't remember being this excited about seeing a woman in his life. His hands were sweating. He wiped them against his jeans. What could he expect from Dana? She hadn't tried to contact him.

Hadn't sounded excited to talk to him. Would their dinner be a friendly thing and nothing more? He'd accept friendship if that's all she'd wanted. It would be difficult, but he'd do it.

He pulled up in front of the white clapboard house and stopped. It was neat and tidy, with the shrubbery trimmed and blooming flowers planted along the short brick walkway leading to the steps to the porch. The porch floor and the stairs were painted a dark green along with the screened door. On either side of the door were two wooden rockers. At both ends of the porch were large flowerpots with trailing greenery. The house looked like a home, not just a place to sleep like his was. It made him feel calm just seeing it.

He carried a bouquet of wildflowers and a bag of food. The main door stood open so he knocked on the screen door. His heart beat faster as Dana padded on bare feet toward him. As she drew closer he held his breath. He ached to hold her but he'd control his urge. It seemed like forever since he'd seen her.

His eyes eagerly took her in. She wore a simple pink T-shirt and short cutoff blue jeans that showed those shapely legs that had wrapped around him. His mouth watered. Her hair swung freely around her face. He'd never seen anyone more desirable. What made her even more gorgeous was the smile on her lips despite the unsure look in her eyes.

Opening the screen, she said, "Hello. Come in."

"Hi." He brushed by her on his way inside. That slight contact already had his body coming alive. His blood rushed south. He needed to go slow. Not scare her. Dana might be fearless in the woods but he was well aware she lacked it in her personal life. Part of that was his fault. He wanted to help repair that.

"These are for you." He handed her the flowers.

She smiled. "Thank you. I love flowers."

How did she manage to make something so simple give him such pleasure? "I could tell from your front walk."

"How's your burn? Did you have them look at it at the hospital?" Her focus went to his arm.

"I didn't. But I've had my nurse dress it each day."

Dana nodded. "Good. Come back to the kitchen."

She led him down a short hallway, past a stairway on one side and a living room area with floral-print sofa and cushioned chair, to a large kitchen. It ran along the back of the house that gleamed with white subway tile which had obviously been redone recently. Dana's decor showed her softer side much as her panties had.

He placed the bag of food on the table with the four nonmatching multicolored chairs.

"Thank you." She went to the sink, looked in the space under it and pulled out a vase. Filling it with water, she placed the flowers in, then took time to arrange them before she set them in the center of the table. "Thank you. I really do love flowers."

Travis studied her for a moment. "How're you really doing?"

Her gaze came up to meet his. "I've recovered. Nothing like a few good nights of sleep."

He turned her face so he could see her cheek. "I'm glad. I felt guilty getting you involved in all that. You were great. By the way, Mr. Gunter is on the waiting list for a kidney. Hopefully it won't be a long wait."

"I'm glad to hear that. You were the one who was the good sport during our adventure."

He brushed her cheek with a finger. "I've missed you. Do you think we could extend our temporary arrangement a little while longer?"

"I don't know if that's a good idea."

He took her hand. "In truth, I'm not sure either. But I know I want to see more of you."

Her arms came around his waist. She raised her mouth to his. "I want to see you too."

Travis's mouth met hers. He'd found nirvana once again. He forced himself to keep the kiss light, not gobbling her up as he wanted to.

With a soft sigh, Dana returned his kiss. Her hands traveled over his chest to circle his neck.

He pulled away to nibble behind her ear. She moaned and leaned her head to the side giving him better access. He gladly took it. "You promised me a tour. Do you mind if we start in your bedroom?"

She grinned and took his hand before leading him down the hall. At the stairs, they climbed.

His heart picked up its pace as his manhood grew. "You know what I thought about for the last three days?"

"What's that?" she whispered.

"You, and a nice soft bed."

Dana's heart fluttered. She'd had similar thoughts, as well. It had taken her a day to figure out why Travis hadn't called. He didn't have her number or know where she lived. That put her in a quandary.

Did he want her to call? They agreed on the here and now. Did he want more? Had what they'd shared in the forest just been heated moments and that was it? Should she make up a reason to call him? That, she didn't feel good about. Games weren't her thing. So she'd done nothing.

By the time she'd gotten the message he'd called the station, she'd already started second-guessing what had been between them. At first his voice had sounded terse on the phone, so she'd waited to see where he was headed with the conversation before she became too agreeable. He met her halfway so she'd decided to do her part by inviting him to her house. She had been dying to see him, to touch him, to kiss him.

After stepping just inside her bedroom, she paused. She didn't make a habit of inviting a man to her house. It had been years since she'd done so.

Travis came up behind her, wrapped his arms around her waist and pulled her back against him. His manhood stood tall and ready between them. A shiver went through her, sending blood to her center. She didn't want to give up a moment like this anytime soon. If she could help it.

"Now this I didn't expect. You're such an amazing bunch of contradictions."

By the movement of his head against hers, she could tell he looked around. Dana wasn't sure if that was a good thing or bad. She viewed the room as if seeing it through his eyes. It had ruffled curtains surrounding the two large windows. A brass bed sat catty-corner on one side of the room, covered in a handmade quilt with a floral pattern. Against the headboard were a number of pillows of different sizes. Wall lamps hung on each side of the bed. An overstuffed paisley-covered chair had a home in another corner. Nearby was a large antique chifforobe and a French provincial desk in front of the back window. Bright-colored paintings of different areas within the national forest hung on the walls.

"It's all feminine-looking and yet you act so tough on the outside."

She turned in his arms so she could see his expression. "Is that a bad thing?"

"Hell, no. That's like having the perfect piece of candy, hard on the outside and very gooey and perfect on the inside."

"You called me candy before. I think I'll take that as a compliment."

"It was meant that way." He kissed her temple before his lips traveled down to her neck where he stopped to nibble.

She closed her eyes and enjoyed the touch of his lips. As Travis worked his magic, he walked her backward toward the bed. She gave no resistance. Her fears had been groundless. Travis still wanted her.

"Did I mention how much I like your house? I especially like that big porch across the front. But I'm thinking this may be my favorite room."

"I don't get to spend much time here this time of the year. Mostly I live at the station."

"Tonight I hope I can make you wish you were here more often."

The back of her legs touched the mattress. Her gaze met his.

His eyes had turned a smoky blue. They flamed with desire.

She suddenly felt self-assured and sassy. "How do you plan to do that, Dr. Russell? Do you have some kind of magic wand?"

He rubbed his hips against her. "I think you know that I do."

"Is that all talk or is there going to be any action behind it?"

He gave her a wolfish grin. "I think instead of telling you about my powers I'll show you." His lips took hers in a deep, delicious and determined kiss.

She no longer doubted his desire for her. She had turned into nothing but begging heat. It only became worse when one of his hands cupped her behind while the other one moved over her bare thigh. His finger slipped under the elastic of her panties to brush her curls.

Her center throbbed like a drum. His mouth moved to taste the skin above the top of her shirt. "I like these shorts far better than I do your cargo pants. Sexy, very sexy."

She cupped his cheek. "All nice and smooth. I sort of like that rough manly look."

"I'll keep that in mind." He rubbed his face against her palm.

Dana pulled him to her. Her hands running down his back to the hem of his golf shirt. She wanted to touch his skin. Needed to. Her body sizzled with sensation.

Travis stepped back enough she could remove it. With it gone, he pulled her to him. Her nose buried in his chest.

She inhaled. "You smell so good."

"Not like dirt, smoke and sweat I hope."

"No. You smell like Travis. I remember it from years ago. A smell I'll never forget."

Travis kissed her deeply as if she'd said something very important to him. Breaking the contact, he placed his hands on her waist and lifted her, then fell on the bed with a bounce. He gave it an extra bounce, making her do so, as well. "Nice. I might never leave."

She liked the idea too much but that wasn't the type of relationship they agreed on. "You could be alone much of the time this time of the year."

"Then I need to make the most of now. I'd hate for you to have to run off."

She looked at him sweetly. "What about our supper?"

His mouth found one of her breasts and teased it through the material of her shirt and bra. "I've decided to have dessert first."

"I guess the tour will wait too."

"Uh-huh. I'll see the rest of the house later." He looked up and met her gaze with a grin. "Maybe next week."

CHAPTER TEN

FOR DANA, THE next two weeks passed in a blur of Travis. All she wanted to do was stay in bed with him. Her life had turned into what she'd always dreamed it could be. What she'd always wanted it to be. To have a man in her life she could admire, who made it clear he wanted her and who made her feel special. She felt truly blessed.

Yet she knew that one day soon Travis would call an end to it. They didn't talk about the future. They lived in the moment. She wasn't sure how long she could continue to do that no matter how sweet she found their time together. Commitment was important to her, knowing she belonged. A forever place.

She'd been called out to fight a fire once during that time. For the first time she had not been eager to leave. All the times she left with excitement pumping through her veins. While she'd been gone the excitement had been about returning to Travis. The necessity of sleeping on the cool ground had never bothered her before, but now she knew what it was like having Travis hold her in his strong arms and against his solid body.

He stayed at her house most nights. They were slowly growing into what looked like a real couple. They rose early, made love, then Travis prepared breakfast and they took their coffee out on the porch to watch the sunrise. In the evenings, she cooked dinner. He'd yet to say anything about reading something into that. She wondered more than once if he saw it as the sign of her deep feelings.

One night Travis had to go to his office to see a patient after hours. She joined him. He asked her to help him do vitals as he examined the woman having breathing problems. Dana liked that he appreciated her skills and trusted her.

During their first weekend together they slept late. Travis did some paperwork while she tended to her flowers. With that done, they mucked out the barn and saw to the horses. Travis acted eager to help, and just as he had in the forest, took her direction. That evening they went to dinner at a local restaurant. As far as she was concerned they'd been wonderful days.

In the middle of their second weekend Travis said, "I have a medical association dinner to attend next Saturday night. I'd like you to go with me."

Such a fancy meeting wasn't her usual type of event. Growing up with just her grandfather who didn't do much socializing outside of church on Sunday, she didn't know much about being social. Even her prom she'd missed. Not because she wasn't asked but because she knew her grandfather didn't have the money for a dress. "Those really aren't my thing. I don't have anything to wear."

"All you need is something nice. Nothing fancy."

That sounded just like a man.

"As far as I'm concerned you look good in anything." He grinned. "But look your best in nothing."

She gave him an appalled glance and lightly slapped his arm. "I'm sure everyone would appreciate that."

"Please come with me, Dana. It's just dinner." His eyes pleaded. That look she had a difficult time resisting. "I'd really like you to come with me."

How could she say no? "I'll see if I have a dress or a nice pants outfit I can wear."

"If you decide to buy one or the other let

me get it for you." He wore that begging look again.

She liked that Travis wanted to do something nice for her. "You don't have to do that."

"I know, but I'd like to."

The idea of letting him care for her didn't fit her usual independent personality. But this time she would let him have his way. Still it niggled at her that she had no idea where this relationship was going.

The night of the dinner meeting Travis decided to dress at his condo. He said he wanted to make their evening out be like a date.

Dana had bought a new dress. A summer-sky-blue color, it was a simple shift with no sleeves. Nothing fancy. She splurged for a pair of silver sandals and had taken the time to have her hair trimmed. Going through her small jewelry box, she located the necklace and matching bracelet that had been handed down to her by her mother and put them on. The only things she owned that showed they might have cared.

Looking at herself one way and then the other in the full-length mirror, Dana had to admit she looked her best. That gave her confidence for the evening. The fact she'd be with Travis who was such a stunning man helped, as well. She had no doubt he'd take care of her and not leave her to fend for herself.

When she opened the door for Travis, he just stood there staring at her, as if stunned. Growing self-conscious, she touched her hair.

"You look absolutely gorgeous."

"You don't look half bad yourself." Unable to resist touching him, she ran her hands down the lapel of his black suit. He wore a blue shirt that matched his eyes and a tie of the same, striped blue and black. To say he looked dashing would've been an understatement. "I don't think there'll be a better looking man there."

"And I may get in a fight because all the men are looking at you."

She smiled. "That's not likely to happen."

He offered her his arm and helped her down the front steps, opened the car door to his late-model luxury car and saw her settled inside.

As they made the circle in front of the country club, Dana said, "I've never been here before. Heard about it, but not been here." She hated places like this, felt intimidated by them.

A valet attendant saw to the car. Travis escorted her to the door. The moment they stepped inside the building someone called Travis's name. He directed her over to the man. With his hand at her waist, which gave her reassurance, he introduced her. Travis made small talk for a minute and they continued down a large open hallway. Others spoke to him and in each instance he took the time to make sure she met them. For someone who had moved back to town fairly recently and been gone for a number of years, he knew a lot of people.

They kept moving until they entered a large banquet room. People mingled with drinks in their hands and around dining tables set for a meal.

Paying more attention to the women than the men, Dana was relieved to see she had dressed correctly. She didn't have to look hard because most of the women in the room were looking at Travis. He was without a doubt the best-looking person there. She smiled. He was hers. For tonight.

"Why the frown?"

She pushed the thought away and forced a smile. "I didn't know I was."

"Would you like a drink?" Travis asked.

"A white wine would be nice."

Travis left her and went to the bar. She looked around the room filled with well-dressed people. All the women seemed to have manicured fingernails and fashionable hair-cuts. She knew her hair was more functional than stylish and her nails were cut short with no polish.

This wasn't a group she fit into. Travis needed someone who belonged in his world. How long would it be before he realized that? She looked at him. Her heart would break when he realized it and left her.

A plump woman with short curly brown hair approached. "Hi. I'm Doris. You must be Dana. I'm Travis's nurse."

"Oh. Hello."

"It's nice to meet you. Travis can't say enough about you. You've made him smile. I like that. He came to town far too serious and sad."

Dana wasn't sure what to say. "Thank you."

"He talks about you constantly. He's crazy about you."

Heat went up Dana's neck yet she liked hearing that. She was certainly crazy about Travis. Too much so. She had stepped past her promise to herself not to get too involved with him. She was destined for hurt.

"I fully expected you to be wearing a Wonder Woman outfit." Doris looked her over. "Lovely dress."

"Thank you. It can't be that bad?" What in the world had Travis been saying?

Doris gave her a knowing grin. "Oh, yeah. It's nice to see you're a mere mortal."

"I can assure you that I am." Dana had to get the conversation going in a different direction. "Are you the nurse who took care of his burn?"

"I am." The woman nodded.

Dana leaned toward her like she planned to tell a secret. "Then you know he's a much better doctor than he is a patient."

Doris laughed, one that made her eyes squint.

Travis returned, then handed the wineglass to Dana. She took a sip.

"I see you've met, Doris."

Doris gave him an angelic look. "Yes, we were having a little girl talk about you."

Dana grinned at Travis's stricken look. "Should I be worried? I don't need my nurse and my...uh friend ganging up on me."

Dana's stomached tightened. Travis didn't even know what to call her. What was she to him anyway? A longer-than-usual fling?

A man not much taller than Doris came up beside her. "This is my husband, Sheldon."

"Hello," he said to both Dana and Travis.

The men shook hands.

Her husband put his hand on Doris's shoulder. "I'd like for you to come met someone."

"Okay." She looked at her and Travis, "we'll see you later then."

She and Travis nodded then wandered around the room for the next fifteen minutes speaking to different couples Travis knew. As people started finding their tables, they located theirs, as well. Three other couples joined them.

Travis knew all of the men. They worked at the hospital. They introduced their wives and Travis saw to it she was introduced, as well. As they ate dinner, Dana remained perfectly happy to eat and listen to the conversations around her.

They were being served dessert when the woman sitting next to her asked, "Dana, what's it you do for a living?"

Dana hesitated for a moment then she squared her shoulders. She had a job to be proud of. Just because historically it was a man's profession and dirty didn't mean it was any less important. "I'm a smokejumper."

The woman's eyes widened and she looked at her as if she wasn't sure how to respond. "Like one of those people who jumps out of an airplane into the forest to put out fires?"

"Yes, I'm one of those."

"That's amazing." The woman sounded as if

she meant it. She turned to her husband. "Did you hear what Dana does for a living?"

"No."

She told him loud enough it got the entire table's attention.

Travis ended his conversation with the man on the other side of him and turned toward her, putting his arm across the back of the chair.

"I've watched news stories about people who do your type of work," one man said.

Travis squeezed her shoulder. "Dana's the best. She also has an advanced EMT and Wilderness First Responder certificate."

Was Travis trying to make them believe she belonged in their world by selling her qualifications? Thankfully the spotlight was taken off her and turned to focus on a man who had come to the podium in the front of the room.

She looked at Travis unsure of what his reaction had really been to everybody's response to her job. He gave her a smile of reassurance. Over the next hour a number of people spoke, giving reports. She wasn't interested, nor did she even understand, but she listened patiently. She would really have liked to go home.

Under the table, Travis put his hand on her thigh. She squirmed. When he brushed his thumb upward, her center tingled. The man just did something to her.

They were on their way out when a snow-white-haired man stopped Travis. "Can I speak to you alone for a moment?"

Travis looked at her.

She nodded. "I'll wait for you in the lobby."

The two men stepped off to the side. She continued on down the hall to the front of the building. She took a spot beside one of the large windows near the main entrance. She watched as the attendants worked bringing cars to those who waited. Glancing at her watch, she checked the time and looked up when there was a flash of lightning. Her crew was due up next for a jump.

She heard a female voice say, "Can you believe that she's a smokejumper, of all things!"

Dana turned to see who spoke.

A tall, leggy woman with red hair and long fingernails done with French tips had her back to her. She stood with another woman.

The red-haired woman continued, "She looks nothing like what I expected Travis to be interested in. When we dated he gave me the impression he was looking for a woman who wanted a good time, not hearth and home. Maybe he's just playing with her like he played with me."

"I thought she was lovely and certainly more interesting than the usual people that attend this dinner," the other woman said before she walked out the door toward the cars.

Seconds later Travis joined her. "Sorry I took so long." He kissed her temple. "Henry was asking me to consider being an officer in the medical association."

"That sounds important. Do you want to?"

"I told him I needed to think about it." He led her toward the door. "It always looks good on your vita to be an officer in an association. That alone makes it tempting."

They joined the line to wait on the attendant. The same woman who had been talking about her stood in front of them.

She turned with a smile on her face. "Hello, Travis. How have you been?"

"Marlene, it's nice to see you."

Marlene looked at Travis as if he was dessert and she'd missed it. She ignored Dana.

Travis's arm came around Dana's waist and he pulled her close to his side. "Marlene, I'd like for you to meet Dana Warren."

"Hello, Marlene." Dana offered her hand to Marlene but she didn't take it, her eyes never leaving Travis. As hot as the weather was, there was frost in the air.

Travis continued as if he didn't feel the undercurrent. "Marlene and I met when I first moved back to town. She's a pediatrician."

The implication was they had dated. "That's nice."

Travis nodded his head to the right. "Marlene, I believe that's your car."

A sleek red two-seater sports car pulled up.

"There's ours." Travis led Dana away.

"It's good to see you again," Marlene called.

Travis said nothing as if he hadn't heard her.

As they made their way to the car, Dana said, "I'll take it you two have some kind of history."

"A very short and unillustrious one."

"Is that so?" She watched Travis closely.

"She's a barracuda and I'm not interested in a fish."

Dana couldn't help but chuckle. It was an adequate description of the woman.

"I much prefer a different type of woman. She was far too much like my ex-wife, only interested in the status she thought two doctors together could bring her. She liked that idea far better than me. She didn't take me breaking it off with her well."

Dana stomach dipped. Would that be how it ended with them? "Is that so?"

He looked at her. "I told her up front. She'd didn't want to believe me."

Wasn't that what was happening with her? She'd started to believe there could be more. She needed to get out before he decided it was time he did.

Travis let out a self-satisfied sigh. The evening had gone well. Dana had been a perfect partner. He had known she'd had some major reservations about attending. He understood where her self-esteem issues came from, but by now couldn't she see the successful person she had become? A smokejumper, the best of the best in her profession. She ran her own crew. Owned her own ranch. So why the insecurity?

The very idea she worried she wouldn't know how to act in a social situation he found laughable. She'd proven herself tonight. She might have been uncomfortable at first, but her fears had been groundless.

He took her hand and brought it to his thigh. She'd turned quiet. "It wasn't so bad was it?"

"No. It wasn't so bad." Dana sounded like she meant it. "It's not something I want to do every night."

"There's only one thing I wanna do every night." He looked at her and wiggled his brows.

She laughed. That amazing sound he liked so much. The one that made him feel good about life.

Silence settled over them. A few minutes later Dana asked in a soft voice, "Travis, what're we doing?"

A note in her voice made his chest tense but he kept his response lite. "What do you mean? We're on the way to your house."

"No." Her tone sharpened. "You know what I mean. This relationship. We don't make sense."

"Sense? What doesn't make sense?"

"You're a doctor. I'm a smokejumper. We're not even in the same world."

"Lots of people don't work in the same world. I don't see the problem." He was confused about where the conversation was headed.

"Travis, you live in a different world than I do. Like tonight, you have fancy dinners to go to. I eat MREs. I sleep on the ground. You like a luxury mattress. We just don't make sense."

He shook his head. "Those things don't really matter."

"But you hold a position in town. You've been asked to be a member of the medical board. I'm not the right woman for you. I don't do social functions or fancy events."

"That's garbage. You did just great tonight. What's this all about?" Travis navigated the drive grateful they were home where he could see her eyes. When had he started thinking of her house as his home? That sounded too much like permanency. That wasn't what he'd intended. Loose and easy had been the plan.

"I just think we need to stop this before it gets out of hand. Like eight years ago you wanted one thing and I needed another. It's no different now."

He pulled to a jerking stop before her front door, turned off the car and shifted so he could look at her. The porch light gave him enough illumination to see her expressions. "But we've been having a good time together. We're good together and you know it."

"Sure we are. Hiding out here together. In bed."

"That works for me."

Dana sighed. "Yeah, but we're both hiding from life. You because you're afraid to trust yourself to really care again. For anyone. You do know I'm nothing like your ex-wife, don't you?"

"Of course I do."

"But you can't get past what she did to you. Your plans for your life didn't work out, so now you don't intend to ever make plans with anyone else." Dana put her hand on his upper arm. "We've found friendship again. I want to keep that. I fear if we don't step back now that we might lose it. I don't want that to happen."

"Aren't you borrowing trouble? Looking for something to worry about."

The crackling of lightning off in the distance mirrored their discussion.

"I thought I could do easy, no attachments. But I can't. I'm sorry. I should've never let this get out of hand."

His world had started to crumble. He wasn't sure what he wanted but he didn't want this. Yet what Dana said was true. The longer they were together the more difficult it would be for them to break things off without her getting hurt. He'd hurt her once and he didn't want to do it again. He brushed her jaw with a finger. "Maybe you're right."

She leaned into his hand for a moment, then pulled away. "It has been sweet while it lasted. We had a…what's it called…? Foxhole experience. That's all it ever was."

"If that's the case what do you call the last two weeks?"

Dana hung her head. "A fling. It's time we let it go. While we can look back on it…fondly."

"I can think of other adjectives I'd use. May I call you sometime?"

Dana's lips tightened. Gloom filled her eyes. "Maybe one day. You know you shouldn't depend on anyone for your happiness. I, of all people, know that. I hope that one day you can learn to trust your judgment about people, take a chance on them. Just know they may still disappoint you. Remember when we talked about making mistakes."

Annoyance welled in him. She spoke as if he was the one with all the issues. He wasn't the only one in the car who needed to examine their life. "You might want to spend a little time on yourself, as well."

She straightened until her back pressed against the door. "What exactly does that mean?"

"It means that you've spent so much of your life being rejected that you think everyone is going to. You're harder on yourself than anyone is on you. Your house has to be perfect. You fear everyone is judging you and you'll be found lacking. That makes it impossible to measure up to your expectations."

"That's not true."

He gave her a direct look. "Are you sure about that?"

"Now you're not being fair."

"How's that? By telling you a few home truths? You might just miss that one person who'll never leave you because you won't give him a chance to prove it."

She glared at him then said, "I think on that note I should say good-night. I'll pack your stuff. You can pick it up or I'll stop by your office and leave it with your receptionist."

"Dana," he stepped out of the car as she ran up the porch steps. He went no farther. Maybe it was best this way. A clean cut. Those always healed faster.

On the plane to a fire Dana closed her eyes and thought back to the discussion she and Leo had had the day before when he'd called her into his office.

Shut the door and have a seat.

She did as he asked and pulled a chair up in front of his desk. Leo had already sat in his chair.

He crossed his arms on the desk and fixed her with an unwavering look. *I'm the closest thing you have to a father now and I want to know what's eating you.*

Haven't I been doing my job? She didn't want to talk about Travis.

You know you have. The others have nothing but great things to say about your leadership. But something's not right with you. You haven't been the same for the last month or so. I know you don't share much about your private life but does it have something to do with Dr. Russell?

She pushed to the edge of the seat. *Why would you think that?*

Because for a few weeks after you came back after that trip you walked around with a smile on your face and then one day it was gone. Now you look like you have lost your best friend. You want to talk about it?

Not really. If she did she might break down and sob. She couldn't have that.

I can't make you. I can tell you that I'm here if you need me.

She stood. *I appreciate that.*

Dana had made it to the door when Leo stopped her. *Just so you know, I did a little checking on Dr. Russell before and after your trip. He's one of the good ones. Someone you can trust. Keeps his word.*

I know.

She did. Travis had proved that more than once. When he'd helped put out fires, seen to Mr. Gunter and Ted, not taken advantage of her in the cave and saved her life in the stream. The list could go on.

Had Travis been right? Had she broken it off with him because she feared he'd one day leave her and move on? Yet he hadn't acted like he was interested in leaving her. Had he changed his mind about what he wanted? What if they could've had something real together and she hadn't given it a chance out of fear?

Travis had shown himself to be steadfast and dependable. Even years ago he had been true to his beliefs. Wasn't that someone she was looking for in her life? She'd had that and thrown it away. Travis deserved better. Had earned her trust. A chance to prove himself. She wanted to give him that opportunity. When she got back from this jump she would call him. Ask him for another chance.

"Five minutes," the spotter called.

She'd trained for these moments. The cutting pain in her throat and nose. The burning in her eyes from the boiling smoke. Soot flying around her, into her mouth and nose despite the material covering them. The gasping for breath. The push to stop the express train of panic coming at her. *Can't breathe.* She was going to die if she didn't get some help.

She reached for her radio, pushed the button but the words wouldn't come out of her smoke-filled throat. Waving her arms, she tried to get the attention of one of her crew. He didn't look her direction. She stepped toward him. Stars swam in her eyes. If she went down it would be over. They were in the middle of the forest. She needed to take a breath. And another.

Dana forced herself to keep moving until she could grab the sleeve of the crew member. Her fingers slowly let go as she dropped to the charred ground.

She'd never see Travis again. Never feel his touch. Never kiss his lips. Never be able to tell him she wanted him, how much she loved him. Never...

Over the last month Travis had learned he'd been wrong. Terribly wrong. Some clean wounds were difficult to heal. He'd adjusted to his divorce with less pain than he'd experienced with trying to get over Dana. She'd permeated his life.

Even when he took care of patients, thoughts of how they had worked together to see to Mr. Gunter and Ted popped in his mind. The worst was when he watched the news or heard on the radio about a fire burning in the national park. The first thing he wanted to do was call Dana and see if she was all right. It required a great deal of effort for him not to.

During one of his weekly calls to check in with his mother she asked, "Travis, what's going on?"

"What do you mean? I just told you about my week." He ran his fingers through his hair.

"I mean you haven't sounded like yourself the last few weeks. What has happened?"

Did he dare let that floodgate open? "You remember that year between college and med school?"

"Yes. You always seemed so happy when you called."

"I did?"

She chuckled. "You did. I figured there might be a young woman involved."

"There was. I saw her again a few weeks ago." He went on to tell her most of what had happened between him and Dana.

"What're you going to do?" How like his mother to cut to the heart of things. She and Dana shared that quality.

"I don't know. I afraid she'll want something I can't offer." Why must this be so hard?

"Like what? Love and companionship. Support and caring. The things we all want."

"But I messed up before, thought I had the perfect one, the perfect life planned out."

"Maybe that's the problem. No one's perfect. Life, love is about taking chances. Can be messy. This Dana sounds like she challenges you, can be a partner not a trophy. She's her own person who isn't dependent on you to make her way." His mother lapsed into silence. "By the way, I never thought Brittney was the right person for you."

"Why didn't you say so?"

"Would it have made a difference?" she asked quietly.

It wouldn't have. Back then he thought he knew what he needed.

His mother had given him much to think about. Over the next few days he rolled all she'd said over in his mind, and what Dana had said, as well. The way she saw him. In the beginning he denied it, but the more days that went by the more he thought Dana was right. He'd let Brittney, his lost dreams and his divorce color his life. His ex-wife was gone and done with, yet she still had control over him. That realization made him the sickest.

He needed to talk to Dana. Tell her how he felt. Beg her to open that big heart of hers and let him in. There his heart would be valued and protected. Let her know he trusted her like no other person in his life. She'd have his back and he would have hers. They'd learn to deal with their future and leave the past where it belonged, behind them.

The next day he was seeing a patient when his cell phone buzzed. He ignored it. When it immediately rang again he looked at his patient and said, "Excuse me a minute." He stepped out in the hall.

The number calling he didn't recognize, but he answered anyway.

"Dr. Russell."

"It's Leo Thomas with the Redmond Smoke-jumpers. I thought you'd want to know. Dana is being airlifted in to Redmond Hospital."

Travis leaned back against the wall, fearing his heart might stop. "I'm on my way."

Doris stood at the other end of the hall watching him. As he ended the call she met him. He explained what had happened and that he'd be leaving after he finished with this patient, with no plans to return.

The helicopter carrying Dana hadn't arrived by the time he'd gotten to the hospital. For the few minutes he spent in the ER waiting, he walked back and forth in front of the doors he'd been told she'd come through. Leo arrived soon after Travis did. He looked as tight-lipped and worried as Travis felt.

The second Dana rolled through the doors, Travis was beside her stretcher. She was unconscious. An oxygen mask covered her nose and mouth. He followed her into an examination room. Fortunately, he had made friends with the ER attending, otherwise he would've been sitting in the waiting room.

Travis made sure to stay out of the way so he wouldn't be asked to leave. In the state he was in there was no way he would've been rational enough to handle Dana's care. By the time they moved her up to a room, he was almost beyond reasoning with.

Leo pulled him aside and told him to get a grip, that it wasn't good for him and it wouldn't be for Dana either. Travis handled traumas numerous times as a doctor and held his emotions with no trouble, but this time it was Dana. He stepped out into the hall and composed himself, determined to remain cool in front of Dana when she woke, and she had to wake.

He loved her. That's what she'd been wanting to hear from him. He'd been too afraid to admit it to himself or her. If he didn't take the chance on telling her, he'd walk around half alive for the rest of his life. What he knew now was that he'd take all of her he could have for as long as he could have it. He wouldn't let his past rule his life any longer. He wanted to live large and that meant having Dana beside him. As soon as he could, he'd tell her.

Twelve hours later the greatest of his fears washed away when he saw Dana's eyes flutter, then open. She would live. Still there was a chance her lungs might be permanently damaged. Doctors wouldn't know if there was any major damage for a few more months. He'd be there for her if that was the case. If not, he'd live with her continuing to jump. They would make their life together work. What he'd never do was ask her to give up her job, just as she'd never ask him to give up medicine.

The second time she opened her eyes, Dana looked more like herself. Her eyes were brighter and more aware. He gave her hand a gentle squeeze. "I'm right here, sweetheart."

Her hand tightened on his briefly before her eyes closed.

Dana woke again in the early hours of the morning. The lights were low. She needed less oxygen now but he knew her throat had to feel like it had a raging fire in it. It'd be a while before she could talk; even then her voice might be hoarse.

A nurse brought in a small dry-erase board, telling him Dana shouldn't speak. She could use the board to write what she wanted to say. He had to promise he'd see that Dana used it.

Somewhere close to daylight he stepped out of the room to get a cup of coffee. Returning, he found Dana awake and watching him. He smiled. "Hello, sweetheart."

Her mouth made a movement like a smile but the mask made it hard to tell.

He hoped he was reading her expression correctly.

Dana took a deep breath. Air flowed easier now. But it hurt like the devil to breathe. If she stopped maybe the pain would too. The whoosh of air filled her ears as she exhaled. Something cupped her nose and mouth. She reached for her neck but her hands wouldn't move.

"Sweetheart, don't struggle," someone said near her ear. "Easy."

She knew that voice. The calm, caressing one. *Travis*.

He continued to talk to her. His voice flowed over her. "You're gonna be just fine. Take deep breaths. In, out, in, out. Slowly. I'm right here. I'm not leaving."

His fingers brushed her forehead. She recognized his touch. The one she'd missed so much.

"In and out. In and out."

She coughed leaning forward, pain assaulting her chest.

"Easy, sweetheart." Caution and fear filled Travis's voice.

She listened to his gentle voice in her ear and returned to sleep.

The next time she woke, her eyes flashed open to bright light. Where was she? She looked wildly around. The voice. She wanted Travis's voice. Where was it?

"Hey, sweetheart."

Dana instantly calmed. It still hurt to breathe. Her gaze met Travis's cool refreshing blue one.

"Don't try to talk." He stood beside her and smiled but it didn't reach his eyes. Instead anxiety filled them. His look moved over her as if he was studying her from a doctor's point of view. "I know your throat hurts. I need you to breathe deeply but slow and easy. It won't be long before you'll be able to talk so save it for right now. Okay? Please for me."

She considered him a moment. The lines were deeper around his eyes than they had been. His hair looked as if he'd run his hands through it more than once. Even his clothes looked slept in.

Dana would do anything for him. She nodded.

He kissed her forehead. "Just keep breathing for me, okay. In and out. In and out."

Slowly she returned to the blissful world of sleep. And dreams of him.

She woke to low lights the next time. She looked down to see a dark haired head resting on the side of the bed. Travis held her hand as if she were a lifeline. He softly snored. She tried to speak but no sound came out. A fresh puff of air in her lungs was welcome but it didn't decrease the pain.

As she flexed her hand slightly Travis's head jerked up. His gaze immediately meeting hers. She reached for the mask but he stopped her. He held her hand, kissing the palm.

"Sweetheart, you still can't remove the mask. You need the oxygen. I need you to stay calm and breathe deeply. You've a case of smoke inhalation." He hung his head and shook it as if what he had to say was unbearable. "I… I…uh…almost lost you."

She didn't miss the moisture making his eyes glassy.

"And I need you to stay here with me." His eyes and words pleaded. "I don't want you to talk. I want you to listen. I'll tell you what happened. Squeeze my hand to let me know you understand."

She did as he asked.

"If you have any questions afterward then maybe you can write them down, okay?"

Dana nodded slightly and he smiled.

"You were fighting a fire. A burst of wind came up and created a tornado of smoke. You were right there in it. You were already overcome but you found a crew member. You passed out and were life-flighted out. You've been here for three days. You're doing very well. But you still have a way to go. The more you follow the directions the quicker you'll get out of here."

She pointed to him.

"How did I know you were here?"

She nodded.

"Leo called me when they were bringing you in. I've never been so scared in my life." He took a deep breath, looking as if he was trying to compose himself. "Do you have any questions?"

She shook her head.

"Then close your eyes and sleep. That's the best thing for you. I'll be here when you wake. I promise."

Dana didn't doubt his words. He had been there for her before. He was here now.

The next time she woke, the sun shone through the window and an older nurse stood beside her bed. The mask had been removed and all she wore was an oxygen cannula under her nose. She looked around the room.

"Are you looking for that handsome Dr. Russell?"

Dana nodded.

"I sent him home for a bath and clean

clothes. He's not going to be happy you woke and he wasn't here. He's been here almost four days and it was time he took a break. Why don't we get you cleaned up some so you'll look your best when he gets back?"

Dana gave her an eager nod.

When Travis returned, Dana sat up in the bed with her hair combed and a clean hospital gown on, eating ice chips.

"Travis." His name came out low and hoarse.

He hurried to the bedside, then set his coffee down on the table. Dana reached out her hand and he took it, kissing the top then bringing it to his cheek. "You still shouldn't talk."

"I'm going to."

"I'm sorry. If you need to say anything you need to write it on this board."

Dana shook her head, picked up the board and marker and tucked them under her pillow. "This time I'm the boss inside."

Travis grinned. "Okay."

"I have to tell you this." The words came out stronger.

She looked at him with unsure eyes but smiled.

The tightness in Travis's chest eased. With the way they had left things, he had been afraid she'd tell him to get out.

"I was wrong." She coughed.

"Let's save this for later."

She shook her head. "No, now. I've lived my entire life with people leaving me. You were right. I pushed you away because I was afraid you'd one day leave me too. I don't care how long you stay but that you just let me be a part of your life. Sometime I have to stop running and take a chance. I want to take that on you. Even if it's just on friendship."

"Sweetheart, you weren't the only one who was wrong. I've let my past rule my life. I'm not going to do that anymore. It's time for me to live my best life. And I know that is with you, if you'll give me a chance."

She smiled broadly and nodded.

Travis leaned down and kissed her lightly. "By the way, I love you."

She cupped his cheek. "And I love you."

His heart flipped, then flopped, and raced like an express train. He took her hand and kissed her palm. "Will you marry me?"

"Yes."

"Maybe we can honeymoon at the fire tower. With a good air mattress, of course."

She smiled. "Sounds perfect."

* * * * *